magical★explorer

Reborn as a
Side Character
in a Fantasy Dating Sim

3

"That will be quite impossible, Yukine... Because the one claiming the title of strongest will be moi."

Shion Himemiya

Serves as ceremonial vice-minister of the Ceremonial Committee. Always clad in a kimono instead of her uniform. Her strength is on par with the other main heroines.

"Yukine, Shion, are you forgetting that I'm standing right here?"

Fran
Serves as vice president of the Student Council. An extremely earnest and diligent girl. She sees Yukine and Shion as her rivals.

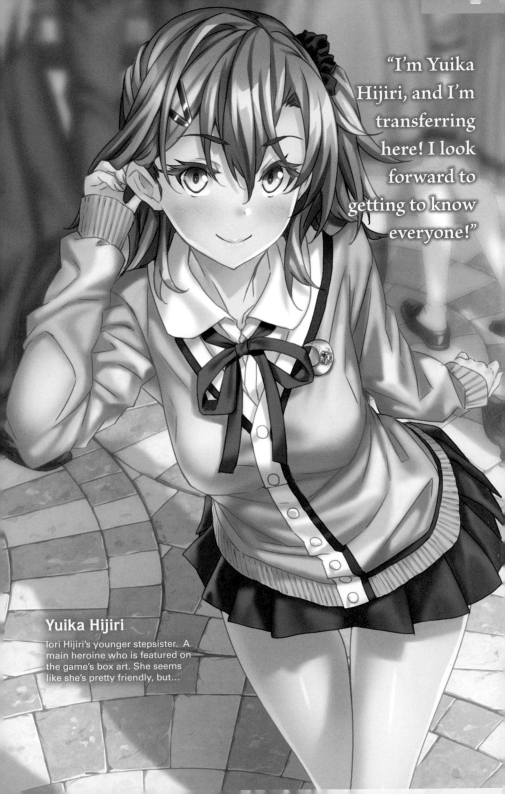

"I'm Yuika Hijiri, and I'm transferring here! I look forward to getting to know everyone!"

Yuika Hijiri

Iori Hijiri's younger stepsister. A main heroine who is featured on the game's box art. She seems like she's pretty friendly, but...

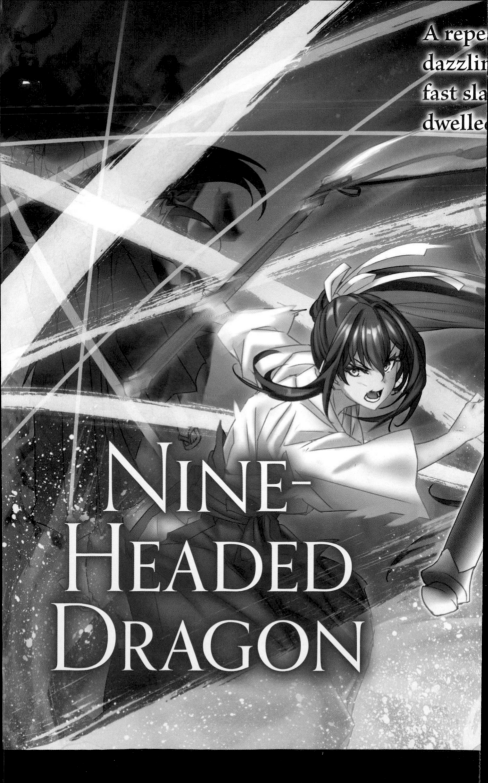

A repe
dazzlin
fast sla
dwelle

NINE-
HEADED
DRAGON

ated series of
ng, lightning-
shes. In each
d a dragon.

Yukine Mizumori

One of the officially recognized
overpowered characters who are
collectively referred to as the Big Three
of *Magical★Explorer.* Lieutenant of the
Morals Committee.

Magical★Explorer

— Volume 3

Reborn as a
Side Character
in a Fantasy Dating Sim

Iris

ILLUSTRATION BY
Noboru Kannatuki

YEN
ON

New York

Magical★Explorer: Reborn as a Side Character in a Fantasy Dating Sim, Vol. 3

Iris

Translation by David Musto
Cover art by Noboru Kannatuki

This book is a work of fiction. Names, characters, places, and incidents are the product of the author's imagination or are used fictitiously. Any resemblance to actual events, locales, or persons, living or dead, is coincidental.

MAGICAL★EXPLORER Vol.3 ERO GAME NO YUJIN KYARA NI TENSEI SHITAKEDO, GAME CHISHIKI TSUKATTE JIYUNI IKIRU
©Iris, Noboru Kannatuki 2020
First published in Japan in 2020 by KADOKAWA CORPORATION, Tokyo.
English translation rights arranged with KADOKAWA CORPORATION, Tokyo through TUTTLE-MORI AGENCY, INC., Tokyo.

Yen On
150 West 30th Street, 19th Floor
New York, NY 10001

Visit us at yenpress.com ★ facebook.com/yenpress ★ twitter.com/yenpress ★ yenpress.tumblr.com ★ instagram.com/yenpress

First Yen On Edition: September 2022
Edited by Yen On Editorial: Maya Deutsch
Designed by Yen Press Design: Liz Parlett, Andy Swist

Yen On is an imprint of Yen Press, LLC.
The Yen On name and logo are trademarks of Yen Press, LLC.

The publisher is not responsible for websites (or their content) that are not owned by the publisher.

Library of Congress Cataloging-in-Publication Data
Names: Iris (Light novel author), author. | Kannatuki, Noboru, illustrator. | Musto, David, translator.
Title: Magical explorer / Iris ; illustration by Noboru Kannatuki ; translation by David Musto.
Other titles: Magical explorer. English
Description: First Yen On edition. | New York, NY : Yen On, 2021–
Identifiers: LCCN 2021039072 | ISBN 9781975325619 (v. 1 ; trade paperback) | ISBN 9781975325633 (v. 2 ; trade paperback) | ISBN 9781975325657 (v. 3 ; trade paperback)
Subjects: CYAC: Video games—Fiction. | Role playing—Fiction. | Magic—Fiction. | Fantasy. | LCGFT: Light novels.
Classification: LCC PZ7.1.I76 Mag 2021 | DDC [Fic]—dc23
LC record available at https://lccn.loc.gov/2021039072

ISBNs: 978-1-9753-2565-7 (paperback)
978-1-9753-2566-4 (ebook)

10 9 8 7 6 5 4 3 2 1

LSC-C

Printed in the United States of America

Chapter Select

CONTENTS

Magical ★ Explorer

Illustration: Noboru Kannatuki

Graphic Design: Kai Sugiyama (Tsuyoshi Kusano Design Co., Ltd.)

Characters

Magical★Explorer 3

Kousuke Takioto

The best friend character from *Magical★Explorer*. The soul of a Japanese eroge afficionado dwells within him. Possesses a unique ability.

Ludie

Ludivine Marie-Ange de la Tréfle.

Highborn second daughter to the emperor of the elven Tréfle Empire. A main heroine who appears on the game packaging for *Magical★Explorer*.

Yukine Mizumori

One of the officially recognized overpowered characters who are collectively referred to as the Big Three of *Magical★Explorer*. Lieutenant of the Morals Committee.

Marino Hanamura

Principal of Tsukuyomi Magic Academy, the game's main setting. Receives limited screen time in the game, so she's shrouded in mystery.

Hatsumi Hanamura

Marino Hanamura's daughter and Kousuke's second cousin. Generally very quiet and reserved. Teaches at Tsukuyomi Magic Academy.

Claris

Elf who serves as Ludie's bodyguard and maid. Serious and devoted to her mistress, she has a tendency to beat herself up over her failures.

Iori Hijiri

The main character in the game version of *Magical★Explorer*. Ordinary in appearance. When developed, however, he becomes the strongest character in the game.

Rina Katou

One of the main heroines present on the *Magical★Explorer* box art. A competitive spirit who is sensitive about her meager bust.

Nanami

A maid created to assist Dungeon Masters. Belongs to the angel race, who are few in number.

Monica

Monica Mercedes von Mobius.

The president of the Student Council. One of *Magical★Explorer's* Big Three and a main heroine who features on the game's packaging.

Stef

Stefania Scaglione.

Serves as the captain of the Morals Committee. The Acting Saint from Leggenze. Although she is beautiful, compassionate, and popular with the students… is there more to her than meets the eye…?

Benito

Benito Evangelista.

Serves as the ceremonial minister, the president of the Ceremonial Committee. Despised by the students of the Academy, but beloved by eroge players.

Glossary

Magical★Explorer 3

Three Committees

The collective term for the student organizations that wield considerable authority on campus—the Student Council, the Morals Committee, and the Ceremonial Committee. Only an elite selection of the student body can join, so their members comprise the Academy's most powerful and influential attendees.

Student Council

The organization in charge of planning and carrying out events like the school festival and magic tournament. Its members are role models to the rest of the student body.

—

Members:
President: Monica Mercedes von Mobius / Vice President: Franziska Edda von Gneisenau

Morals Committee

The organization that works to protect moral integrity on campus. Whenever a violent incident occurs, they are the primary group to resolve the situation.

—

Members:
Captain (Presidential Role): Stefania Scaglione / Lieutenant (Vice Presidential Role): Yukine Mizumori

Ceremonial Committee

The organization in charge of auditing the Student Council and issuing motions of no confidence against them. It remains uncertain, however, whether they are actually performing their duties.

—

Members:
Ceremonial Minister (Presidential Role): Benito Evangelista / Ceremonial Vice-Minister (Vice Presidential Role): Shion Himemiya

—Yukine's Perspective—

As I walked through campus, exchanging hellos with people along the way, I noticed a boy attracting an unusual amount of attention.

Her wore a red stole, a bit longer than he was tall. Anyone would do a double take if they saw something like that floating idly in the air, as if to avoid touching the ground, while its owner strode through campus. Add to that the beautifully silver-haired maid following closely behind him, and it was almost like he was asking to get stared at.

The looks he attracted were not kind ones, nor were the voices that rose around him cheers.

"Why's he even at school?"

"If he's not motivated, he should just stay home."

I could hear their character assassination all around me.

As far as I could tell, the slander was primarily originating from Lovely Lovely Ludivine, or LLL, a fan club for Ludie.

People were surprisingly simple, and if there was some sort of gossip going around about someone, they would more or less come to view that person through a biased filter. In this case, a filter branding Takioto as an "underachiever," a "shallow dude," and a "troublemaker" was cast over him on account of all the rumors he'd attracted.

Now that those labels had stuck, everything he did screamed "underachiever." All because of this filter.

Unfortunately, it made perfect sense why people saw him that way. After all, Takioto *was* an underachiever, in a sense—he certainly misbehaved, and he did come across as a flippant and shallow guy.

And that's what everyone who perceived him as such thought. That all the rumors were true. The sad reality was that even if the gossip about Takioto was false, it would effectively become fact once the majority of people believed it. That meant Takioto *was* an underachiever.

The group who especially despised him, LLL, was also the original source of that slander. They couldn't stand a deadbeat like him being friends with Ludie. Though some members of LLL urged the group to "respect their lady's wishes," they were in the minority.

The boy in front of me must have been an LLL member, too.

"We should say it to his face, right?" he suggested, scowling.

The two boys acting as his cronies meekly nodded.

I didn't know who these students were. However, I got the sense that the boy who was speaking was a noble from one country or another.

Academy students claimed that everyone here was equal in regard to social standing and citizenship. Thus, while some attendees were of royal or aristocratic background, they couldn't brandish their authority against other students.

Officially, anyway.

The reality didn't quite live up to the ideal. Students from the same nation's aristocracy might already be acquainted with one another prior to matriculation, in which case their relationships would be hierarchical from the start. Plus, it was pretty much impossible to avoid having preconceived notions about classmates who held lofty positions, like princess or Acting Saint. That being said, there were students on campus whose social status was based on merit, like those in the Three Committees.

Nobles could be extremely egotistical, though there weren't many at the Academy. They'd get angry if things didn't go their way and would sometimes lash out at people as a result. That explained how they were treating Takioto at the moment.

With him, their resentment manifested in the glares they shot his way. The insults they threw. On top of that, a growing number had begun shouting at him to stay away from Ludie. Just like this boy who was heading over to give Takioto a piece of his mind.

A part of me felt that the people who acted this way should just settle things with a duel, but first-years were still banned from conducting them. Either way, it was clear that Takioto would crush this guy if they did get into an altercation. It was possible that would only add fuel to everyone's anger toward him. No matter what the people around him thought, though, Takioto was still Takioto.

But I knew better. I knew that Takioto was a reliable person who was worthy of trust. That the more time you spent with him, the more he grew on you.

Just as Takioto said something to Nanami with a look of exasperation on his face, the noble boy from earlier began to close in on him. Takioto glanced over at the student but otherwise ignored him and kept on chatting with Nanami. That was when the boy called out to him. If anything happened, I'd be sure to step in. Or so I'd thought, but my fears proved to be unfounded.

Takioto flashed a look at Nanami to hold her back, then addressed the interloper with his typically flippant smile. This was enough to diffuse the situation despite how incensed the noble had been on his way over. He backed off after hurling a flurry of insults at the two of them.

Then Takioto went back to his conversation with Nanami as if nothing had ever happened. It was probably their usual back-and-forth. They were like a two-person comedy routine.

"Then what about when making omelets? In that case, it's gotta be soy sauce, right?"

"I do agree it is hard to pass on soy sauce, but my everyday go-to is the Nanami Special."

"What the heck's a 'Nanami Special'? C'mon."

"You've never heard of the Nanami Special?!"

"O-of course not! You say that like it's obvious, but I've got no clue what the hell you're talking about!"

When I approached the two of them, Nanami and Takioto both turned to me and smiled.

"Oh, hi, Yukine."

"Good day, Miss Mizumori," Nanami said, holding out a tablet so that Takioto couldn't see. Written on the screen was an explanation of the Nanami Special. She clearly wanted me to go along with her bit.

I knew what she wanted me to say. I felt bad for Takioto briefly, but I decided I'd play along with Nanami for a while.

"If I recall correctly, a Nanami Special is when you let a specially made Nanami extract steep overnight and add it as seasoning to a dish."

"Why do you know that?!"

I couldn't help myself from laughing at his reaction. Of course I wouldn't have any clue about it.

"And besides, what the hell's Nanami extract, some fancy new dietary supplement?!"

"Master, please… Are you really going to make me say it?"

"The real question here is, what about it's got you embarrassed…?"

He had a point—what in the world was Nanami extract? I decided it was best not to pry. I didn't need to rile him up any further.

"Oh well, let her keep her secrets. Haven't seen you since this morning, Takioto. Nice to see you, Nanami."

I got the feeling even more eyes were trained on us. It probably had something to do with me being a member of the Discipline Committee. I urged the two onward, and we began walking.

"What happened with that guy from earlier?"

At my question, Takioto gave a half-hearted reply, as if he couldn't care less.

"He straight up told me I'm a bad influence on Ludie," he said, shoulders slumped.

I'd expected as much. The noble really had seized the opportunity to give Takioto a piece of his mind. He'd said that Takioto's attitude in class was reprehensible, that he didn't attend afternoon classes, and that he was acting however he wanted in class, as if the school was his personal playground. Inconveniencing students who took their studies seriously, essentially.

"What did you think, hearing all of that?"

"He's not completely off the mark. After all, I do skip both my morning and afternoon courses. Still, I don't think I'm going out of my way to bother people."

"What an utterly outrageous victim complex he's got."

Nanami was exactly right.

"But it's all up to Ludie," Takioto continued.

"If she really didn't like me, I'd keep my distance from her, no questions asked. But I trust Ludie, and I get the feeling she has faith in me, too."

Could Ludie count on Takioto? That went without saying.

"I can vouch for that."

"That naturally goes for you, too, Yukine."

"Trust, huh…? Well, you do get out of control every once in a while. Like when Ludie was kidnapped, for example," I said teasingly, prompting a strained smile from Takioto.

"I'm kidding, of course. I trust you, even taking that into consideration."

At this, he smiled a wide, toothy grin. It was a very cute display.

Takioto normally came off as somewhat superficial. In that respect, his demeanor certainly didn't help, but what really sealed the deal was the silly grin he was always wearing. That being said, when it really mattered, his expression would grow solemn. At the end of the day, he was someone who would have your back.

"Oh, right, Yukine," he said, grinning at me.

"I'm making some arrangements to pull off something that'll really surprise you."

Something that would surprise me?

"Honestly, it's gonna be pretty intense. I might end up falling flat on my face trying to accomplish it—that's how difficult it'll be. But I need it so bad that I'll do whatever it takes to get it. I think that's why things have been such a mess for me at school lately. But just you watch, okay?"

He pounded on his chest.

"Watch me from here on out, 'cause I'm gonna be the strongest in the world." He smiled.

I had no idea what he was going to get up to. And even if I asked him about it, I bet he'd just dodge the question.

Takioto had the support of his family, Principal Marino Hanamura and her daughter, Miss Hanamura, along with Ludie, Nanami, and Miss Claris. Looking at him—blessed with such an environment, cognizant of his own talents, and with an almost stubbornly honest work ethic—I could see that he had a bright future ahead of him. It seemed almost too dazzling, like a light shining into my eyes.

Takioto and Nanami walked off together in a separate direction from the school building.

As I watched them leave, it came to me. Though they looked the same as ever, they seemed closer than usual. Had something happened between them? I was picking up on a kind of invisible trust in each other radiating from them both.

"The strongest in the world, is it?"

Continuing to watch him as he walked off, I suddenly thought of my older sister.

"I'm not a genius. If you're so insistent on labeling me a genius, then you need to accept it. You're a genius, too, Yukine."

Maybe talking with Takioto so much was reminding me of my sister. *"You can become stronger than anybody. Believe in yourself. I think you could become the absolute strongest in the world. So set your sights on it."*

"Instead of me...then?"

Eroge protagonists and an extraordinarily fulfilling school life often went hand in hand.

The leading man was destined for friends he could rely on, heroines who adored him, and a narrative where he would succeed. Many eroge players were after exactly that sort of blissful story in the first place, so it made sense it would play out that way.

But how was it for the friend characters in these games?

I'd hesitate to say they always wound up happy. But I figured I could avert that fate by making the right choices, just like the protagonist could.

How was that actually working out for me, you ask?

Well, random nobles from who knows where were trying to threaten me all the time, and on top of that, a portion of the student body couldn't stand the sight of me.

The thing was, I wanted to get stronger no matter what, and to do that, there were some things I really needed to get my hands on. That meant I really didn't have much choice in my activities. In some respects, it was entirely predictable how things were playing out.

But when I thought of my goal, I couldn't care less about the glares from other students. The occasional weird dude trying to pick fights wasn't a problem, either. I'd known that my behavior was going to attract attention anyway. It was bound to happen sooner or later.

Despite the fact that I was developing an awful reputation, my mood was still sunny and bright.

Things were going smoothly. So smoothly, it was laughable.

It wasn't just that, either. I was living such a fulfilling life. I bet it rivaled even the fulfilling existences of the world's eroge protagonists.

Nanami working with me was a huge boon. She had the initiative to take care of things without needing me to ask her, so I was progressing faster than expected. We only had issues during times like these, when she couldn't be at my side, which she complained about nonstop.

I'd already triggered the flag for the next event I had to hit, so now I had to think about what I needed to do next.

I was smack-dab in the middle of heading to the library, mulling everything over, when—

"Why, oh why don't you ever show up for me?!"—I heard someone practically shout at me from behind.

Standing there was a petite, strawberry-blond woman. In addition to her unbelievably charming downward-tilted eyes, complete with a mole beneath, she had a lovely voice that was practically therapeutic.

"M-Ms. Ruija?"

Why was she here all of a sudden? I couldn't help but wonder. As we moved to the Magic Research Lab III and she filled me in on the circumstances surrounding her appearance, I began to understand. If anything, I felt guilty for having done something so awful to her.

Apparently, Ms. Ruija had investigated a number of things regarding my peculiar constitution after we'd agreed to "work hard on this together." But after complaining to Sis about how I never showed up to afternoon classes, she came to learn that we were related and living in the same household.

"Hatsumi was my upperclassman! We ventured into the dungeon together, too," Ms. Ruija explained, looking back fondly.

A personal lesson alone with Ms. Cutie… No, a personal lecture… *Hold on, why does that sound so lewd?*

"Really?"

"We sure did! Wait, did Hatsumi never tell you?"

Now that I thought about it, I hadn't heard anything about her friends at the Academy. To put it rather rudely, she didn't seem to have many… so I thought it would be awkward to ask. She never talked about going out with acquaintances or anything.

"Well for starters, Sis isn't really the type to talk about that stuff."

"That's a good point." Ms. Ruija nodded with a strained smile. "But when the topic turned to you, she actually talked up a storm. For her, anyway."

I couldn't even imagine Sis "talking up a storm."

"It's true, I swear!"

My thoughts were showing on my face, by the sounds of it. But actually, that was enough talk about Sis. I already knew about her, after all. There was something I was much, much more curious about...

"Um, could you maybe explain what this thing is to me now?" I said, pointing at the device.

It was a long, thin tube, with what looked like a suction cup attached to the end. It also vaguely resembled an electrocardiogram machine. There was just something about it. Maybe it was because the tube was attached to an instrument that looked like it was used to forge a pact with a demon from hell, but as I stared at it, I was gripped by nebulous unease.

"This? Can't you tell from looking at it? It's a mana measuring device."

Not at all. I had seen a large variety of devices in the magic tool shops I visited and at the Hanamura household. Even then, I hadn't had a clue.

"Okay then, what're these?"

I pointed to the horns, curled like a sheep's, extending from the side of the machine.

"Those are horns."

I could see that, thank you very much. I wasn't trying to perform some back-and-forth straight out of a beginner's foreign language textbook. I wanted to know what those things were there for.

"Okay, so why does it have them?"

"I don't know."

Unconsciously squatting low to the ground, I put my head in my hands. Then rose again, steeling myself to drop the subject and move on to my next question.

"Here, I get that this machine has a display. But would you explain why the keyboard-looking part below has all those keys with skulls on them? And why it looks like there are a few switches flipped on?"

"I don't know that, either."

"I just remembered I had something urgent to do."

Ms. Ruija latched onto my shoulder as I smoothly turned around to leave.

"No, please don't goooo! I've already checked with Hatsumi that you wouldn't be busy."

Siiiiis! Siiiiiiiiiiiiiiiiiiiiiiiis!

"It's okay. It gave me the creeps when I first saw it, too, but it's fine. I borrowed it from a genius inventor, the most distinguished at the Academy, so it's safe. Totally all right. Probably."

Her reply sounded more like she was trying to convince herself than me. There was one word at the end there I couldn't ignore, either.

"Ms. Ruija, have you tested this machine out yet?"

Please don't avert your eyes so blatantly.

"...By the way, who exactly invented it?"

"You probably don't know her but...Anemone built it."

I reflexively grimaced, then gently put my hand on Ms. Ruija's shoulder and shook my head.

"Ms. Ruija, I'm saying this for your own good—you should give it back to her."

Anemone is a sub-heroine elf the player is guaranteed to befriend to progress through the game. Of all the characters in *Magical ★ Explorer*, she has by far the darkest backstory.

She is also a genius. That is undeniable. Playing off the idea of a mad scientist, fans call her Sexy Scientist or Maso-Scientist; she consistently ranks near the top of the character popularity polls. Anemone and her inventions are a great boon to us eroge-enjoying gentlemen over the course of *MX*, so we use these nicknames with nothing but respect in our hearts.

But true eroge fans think even more highly of her. She is cute, sure, but above all else, they admire her because everything she creates is a wondrous marvel.

That being said, it made no sense for a man to use them. Though an argument could have been made that it'd serve as a nice reward for anyone with feelings for him. *In which case...*

"Don't you think you should test it out first, Ms. Ruija?"

To be perfectly honest with you, I wanted to see it in action.

Unfortunately, she just muttered that it was impossible and slowly backed away from the machine.

"I get nothing but bad vibes from this thing... Besides, she lent it to me after I briefly consulted with her about your condition. That means this device is for you. Not for me. Plus, she promised me she would keep her lips sealed about that thing from before if I tested it out..."

Wait, didn't that sound like a threat?

"Oh, she won't tell anyone, will she?"

"U-uhh..."

Ms. Ruija averted her eyes. Then she fidgeted restlessly, contorting her already tiny body into an even more compact shape.

You're a teacher, aren't you?! Why're you letting a student blackmail you?! is what I wanted to say, but then I recalled that Ms. Ruija's character arc involves being blackmailed. In fact, it's the *Magical ★ Explorer* protagonist himself who has dirt on her.

"...Okay, then. Let's try it... But you have to tell me the whole story."

"Th-that's asking a bit too much..."

"I swear I won't do anything bad with the information."

"W-well, all right, in that case..."

"And thaaaaat's the problem!" I said, unconsciously putting my face in my hands.

"You've already been fooled once, Ms. Ruija. Now do you understand where you went wrong?"

In-game, you don't actually develop your relationship with Ms. Ruija by going to her class. You do need to attend once to trigger her story, though.

Iori receives a brazen invitation from Takioto to "check out a sex shop," and the two hit up a certain store. Of course, it's possible to turn down his offer, but any eroge player is sure to leap at the opportunity, no questions asked.

There, you happen to bump into Ms. Ruija on her first day of work. By the way, Takioto gets kicked out for being rude to another employee, so he doesn't even get to meet her. Truly A+ eroge best friend character behavior.

"I do......"

In-game, Ms. Ruija is strapped for cash and takes up the job in the sex shop part-time. The exact details of her money problems are never made clear to the player, but if the protagonist gives her a huge chunk of change, an amount you won't see until the end of your first playthrough, this starts to resolve the situation. Though at the same time, this puts Ms. Ruija at the protagonist's beck and call, since he can leverage her financial difficulties against her. Now that I thought about it, solving everything with money was quite the power play.

If Ms. Ruija had been more popular with players, the developers might have expanded her storyline in a patch and revealed the source of her duress. Unfortunately, however, she didn't have too many admirers. Though I really liked her, especially because I was a fan of the actress who voiced her. Maybe fans weren't happy the character was so close to thirty?

"I've more or less figured out your situation. But I'd still like you to come clean yourself."

"Oh, well, if you already know what it is, I don't really need to..."

I'm asking because I can't let you out of my sight!

I turned my thoughts into a glare, and Ms. Ruija shrunk back from me.

"S-sorry."

"Oh well, forget it. For now, let's get Anemone's machine working and wrap this up. After that..."

I stared at her pointedly, as if to say, *You know what's coming, right?*

"Y-yes, okay... Hold on, you actually want me to start it up?"

"Anemone is the last person you want getting dirt on you."

Especially since she was a woman. Though I'm sure there were a few guys out there who liked being treated like a dog, so I couldn't really judge.

"Are you really sure about this?" Ms. Ruija asked, looking at me like I was some unbelievable oddity. If she was going to look at me like that, then she shouldn't have been trying to use it in the first place, but that didn't matter at this point.

I took off my stole and jacket, preparing to hook up the suction-cup part of the machine to me. And when I then removed my white shirt, Ms. Ruija let out a sigh of admiration.

"Woooow, incredible..."

Though I was far from the level of a bodybuilder, she reached out to touch my fairly well-toned body. She had been timid at first, but now her hands had grown daring.

"The machine still needs to be prepped, Ms. Ruija..."

"Y-yes, yes, of course. Right away!"

Flustered, she took out what appeared to be the operator's manual and went over it as she finished the preparations. When I peeked at the manual myself, I let out a small sigh.

"......I have to take off my pants, too, huh?"

"P-please."

At this, I loosened my belt, put my hands on my pants, and ripped them down in one swift motion. I glanced at Ms. Ruija and found her covering her face with her hands and peeking at me through the gaps in her fingers.

Was this the latest fad or something? Were all the instructors at the Academy peering at naked bodies through the gaps in their fingers now? First of all, this woman was nearly thirty years old, so I would've appreciated if she didn't get worked up just from seeing a man's bare upper body. Maybe there was a non-zero chance I was actually a stunningly handsome man like you'd find at some pretty-boy entertainment agency?

"Ms. Ruija, I'd like to get this over with quick..."

"S-sorry... *Eek!*" she cried before tripping over her own two feet and slamming into me. Though that was enough to break her fall, Ms. Ruija's hands were now on a very precious part of my body...

"Oh no, oh no, oh no, oh no!"

"*Hngh!*"

Where did this reward come from? I needed to get her off me ASAP before things got *real* bad in all sorts of ways.

"I-I-I'm so sorry!"

Pulling myself together, I attached the suction cup thingamajig to my body. Then, once I finished attaching everything, I gave Ms. Ruija the go-ahead, and the machine started up.

"...A-are you all right?" Ms. Ruija called out to me from a spot several yards away.

"Well, if I had to say one way or the other, I guess I'm all right physically. But mentally, I'm barely hanging on by a thread..."

"I-I'm sorry. B-but still, we were able to collect a good amount of data...!"

"Though we totally destroyed the machine in the process."

I sighed deeply as I watched smoke sputtering out from between the horns on the device.

Sexy Scientist's creation had been as sketchy as I'd anticipated. I didn't even want to think back over it. But with Ms. Ruija at the controls, the machine wasn't the only thing on the verge of bursting—so were my nether regions.

"Hmmm. As far as I can tell, there's something inhibiting you before you try to materialize magic. Or maybe there's something getting in the way?"

"It'd be nice if this led to some sort of solution."

I sighed. Ms. Ruija put her hand to her chin and murmured something else that was on her mind.

"I'm amazed you're able to keep this much mana inside you, Takioto."

"I'll admit, it's a bit of a mystery how it all stays contained within my body."

"Then maybe it's not that your amount of internal mana is abnormal, but that it's being kept in a fundamentally different location? That would lend more credence to the theory of widespread alternate dimensions, along with the alternate dimension preservation hypothesis that Hatsumi proposed. But if that were true, then the magic particles that appear via the spatio-corpuscular magic theory advocated by Faust, which several scholars have partially verified, would be...."

She mumbled, rambling on about something or other.

"Who's to say they aren't both correct, right?" I muttered, not really following any of it.

"If you could prove that, it'd be a huuuuge discovery, one for the history books...," she replied, a serious look on her face.

Well, I wasn't an expert on any of that stuff, so I couldn't really say either way. She'd have plenty of time to think about all that later. With all that settled...

"Okay then, Ms. Ruija. You'll keep your promise now, right?"

I smiled and placed a hand on her shoulder. She jerked her head like an unoiled machine, as though asking whether she really had to. But the answer was obvious.

"Yes."

She stared at me with resignation as she got on the ground and tucked her legs under herself. Then, hands trembling as she gripped her sleeves, she proceeded to relay her problems to me. Just as I'd assumed, it all came down to finances.

As Ms. Ruija put it, she'd somehow managed to lose all her money between various debts and taxes. And somehow, Sexy Scientist had caught wind of the fact that she was planning on taking a part-time job in a sex shop to pay off what she owed. In exchange for her silence, Ms. Ruija would have to do whatever Anemone asked, hence the appalling spectacle just moments prior. Why'd she have to go and tell Sexy Scientist she'd do anything to keep her quiet?

Though to be honest, I was the one who was really bearing the brunt of that woman's machinations at this point.

"Hold on, are you sure you're not being tricked into paying too much back on what you owe?"

I couldn't say anything definitive from her simple overview alone, but the interest rate on her loans seemed mighty fishy. Not to mention the fact that she was paying for things that she'd have been exempt from back in Japan. Maybe this world was just different from where I was from? No, I was positive she was being ripped off.

"Umm, but, according to the person I spoke to..."

"Did you actually look over the contract?"

The more Ms. Ruija explained things to me, the more convinced I became that she was paying for things she shouldn't have been charged for in the first place. In fact, I got the sense someone was taking advantage of her misunderstanding to ratchet up her debt even further. Given how trusting she was, it probably wouldn't be too hard to trick her, either. They were definitely puffing up the interest or reimbursement period to squeeze more out of her.

"Why did you neglect things until they got this bad?"

"Umm, well... Good question."

"...Okay, how old are you again? How many years have you been a productive member of society?!"

"*Eek!*"

I couldn't suppress a sigh as I stared at Ms. Ruija, who was on the verge of tears. I didn't blame her for wanting to cry. One of her students was lecturing *his teacher* on how to be good with money.

"I-I'm sorry."

Another sigh escaped her as she hung her head low to the floor. Now I understood why you needed so much cash in-game to bail her out. But I'd come this far, so I figured I'd help her see things through.

"Take me to your place, Ms. Ruija."

"W-wait, by my place... N-no, you're not planning on capitalizing on my vulnerability to try and have your way with me, are you?!"

"...You've got it all wrong."

"Oh no, no, no, no, no, no, I can't, nooooo..."

This woman was driving me nuts!

"...Gather up your checkbook and other promissory notes you have at your place and hand them over!"

I took out my cell phone and brought up the person I'd been in the most contact with since coming to this world. A woman and a mother. "Oh, Marino? Can you do me a favor and introduce me to an accountant and a lawyer...?"

Marino must've been shocked to hear the request, because her only response was a befuddled "Huuuuh?" Just how old was this lady supposed to be again?

In the end, while Ms. Ruija's debt wasn't completely settled, she was able to get it drastically reduced.

The amount of money she owed had been staggering. The accountant Marino referred me to couldn't even keep a straight face as his jaw hung open in shock, while I had felt ready to throw up on the spot.

Ms. Ruija claimed the loan collectors had put together a monthly peace-of-mind repayment schedule for her, but that repayment plan was pretty horrible in itself; she'd clearly been fooled from the outset. Short of winning the lottery, it would've eventually bankrupted her.

"You're lucky you got through this without selling any organs."

The lawyer was deadpan as he said this, leaving a lasting impression. Incidentally, the organs of capable magic-users fetched a very high price. The real question was what exactly the buyers used them for...

Some of the places we went to get the debt reduced were really scary, but a visit from the lawyers was enough to resolve things. I had to visit an establishment with a particularly shady-looking dude (and was terrified the entire time), but just saying, "I'm Kousuke Hanamura, and the Hanamura family is prepared to fight this—legally and physically," had been enough to take care of it. The genius Hanamura family at work. Though it had been quite the eccentric scene, what with both my legs and the loan shark's trembling in fear.

After listening to the lawyers' report over the phone, Marino and I let out a long sigh as we ended the call.

"I'm having the Hanamura family take on the remainder of her leftover debt in full."

Exhaustion came over her face. She sank deeper into her expensive leather chair and took a sip of her cooled coffee.

"Ms. Ruija couldn't ask for a safer or more dependable creditor..."

According to Marino, Ms. Full-Body Aromatherapy (and Thirty-Year-Old Debt Slave) was a very skilled and powerful magic-user.

"Honestly… Your average instructor would have been let go from the Academy before they could harm its reputation."

"No surprise there…"

For the Academy, it was the obvious way of dealing with the matter. If Ms. Ruija were to lose her position as an educator and the salary that came with it, then after that… It was easy to imagine how she would end up.

At any rate, Marino had handled everything without a single joke or prank, a testament to just how big of a deal the whole situation was. This was the woman who'd still been able to crack jokes when we'd had to force down Sis's Neon-Skyline Dinner Disaster.

"Now it makes sense why Ms. Ruija was living in that dump of an apartment. I had her immediately move into a Hanamura-held apartment building and have ensured that any suspicious characters won't be able to get in. I'm drawing her rent and debt payments straight from her salary. We'll be offering her a repayment plan with a low monthly rate, but unless something major happens, it'll still take her ten years to whittle it all down."

"No surprise there…"

Marino had actually managed to slash the debt to an amount that could be paid off in a decade? That was great news. Though, I didn't think that Ms. Ruija's apartment was as much of a dump as Marino made it out to be. Considering her salary, she'd clearly need a cheap place to live.

"The thing is, I've determined it would be best to have someone to act as her custodian."

"No surprise there."

After everything that had happened, it would be cause for concern if she wasn't placed under someone else's supervision. More than anything else, she was just so easy to fool. Instead of a salary, she'd be better off under an allowance system. If she wanted something, she'd save up her allowance to buy it. No more borrowing money. Wait, how old was she again…?

Marino's somber face broke into a smile. Then she put her hand on my shoulder.

"All right then, Kousuke. I'll leave collecting on her loan and supervising her up to you."

"No surprise there……"

I owed Ms. Ruija for all the times she'd taken care of me in the game, so it only made sense that a true gentleman such as myself should return the favor, especially as a student she was familiar…with… *Hunh?*

"…*Wha—?*"

"Yup! ♪ I knew you'd say that, so I made sure to put your name down on the documents already."

"Whoa, whoa, now hold on a second."

My brain couldn't keep up. Wait, so I was supposed to look after *that*? Marino realized she was asking a student to supervise his own instructor, right?

"You don't need to worry, I made sure to put the apartment building under your name! ♪ The whole building, of course."

"Oh, really? Well, that solves everything! Yeah right, like hell it does!"

I could understand a single apartment, but buying out an entire luxury apartment building must've cost millions! In my past life, I could've worked to the grave and still never earned that much! Though, honestly? That wasn't the important part right now.

"Don't worry, you'll be able to get a lot of use out of a magic-user like her. I don't plan on firing her anytime soon, and I'll be sure to pay her salary."

"Um, so, here's the thing. It's not so much that I'm concerned about the debt, but more that I'm worried about the ethics of this whole thing!"

"Oh, please, it'll be fine! I've already instructed her to give you absolute obedience, for starters. Plus, I made her swear she was mentally prepared for the arrangement, too."

"Ah, gotcha, that's a relief…… Not! All that only makes it even more ethically dubious!"

By "made her swear," Marino meant that she backed Ms. Ruija into a corner, right? She was totally hanging the money over her head and coercing her, wasn't she?

"Anyway, all jokes aside, I've left her debt collection and supervision up to you."

"That's the part I *wish* you were joking about."

She was clearly serious about the most important point in the exchange. I sank into the sofa and, with a deep sigh, took a sip of coffee. All that shouting had made me thirsty.

"That reminds me, you're challenging the Beginner's Dungeon with everyone on Saturday, aren't you?"

"That was the plan."

Ludie had approached me in earnest one day and asked, "How did you get so strong in such a short time, anyway?" To which I had plainly replied, "I've been training in the Beginner's Dungeon." After an invitation to join me, she'd accepted, albeit with some bewilderment. Later, I was surprised to learn that Yukine, Sis, Claris, and even Nanami had all decided to come along. Though I had wanted to bring everyone anyway, so I suppose it had saved me some trouble.

"There's something I'd like to ask of you."

"What's that?"

"You know there's some sort of secret in the Beginner's Dungeon, don't you? Well, for just a little while, I'd like you to keep it under wraps."

I frowned. Why would she use the words "keep it under wraps"? And phrase it as a request instead of an order?

"...You knew about the eleventh layer?"

"Oh no, I had no idea. Why, this is the first I'm hearing about any sort of eleventh layer at all. So there were more than ten after all, huh?"

I didn't know how I was supposed to react to Marino, who seemed completely serious.

"I've already talked about it to Ludie and the others, though...," I added.

"Oh, I'm fine with them; they're all trustworthy."

Was Marino really in the dark about the eleventh layer? I couldn't tell. In times like these, it was best to examine things from a different angle. So assuming she was aware of the secret floor, why did she feel the need to hide it from me right now? What did she gain from doing so?

Personally, I thought the answer was nothing.

"...I didn't mean to go blabbing about it to everyone, but I wasn't shy about it when people asked."

"You don't need to think so hard on it. And I don't really mind if you bring it up, either. That won't cause any problems. I just wanted to clear some things up for myself."

"...Can I ask why?" I inquired, prompting a troubled smile to appear on Marino's face.

"I'm really sorry, but I can't reveal that at the moment. Eventually, the time will come to talk with you and Hatsumi about it. I'd like you to wait until then for me."

I didn't understand... Marino was the head of the Academy, so why wasn't she at liberty to discuss this now? Did she need to run something by someone first? With the Hanamura main family, for instance? Still, shouldn't she be able to give a brief outline to Sis, at least?

"I'd like to let the people I trust know about the secret floor... Do you think you'll take a while?"

I was thinking it would be best to inform Iori's party about how useful the dungeon was. Snagging skills from there was extremely convenient.

"...Hmmm, well, once I get the go-ahead, I'll be able to give you permission straightaway. For the time being, can you just hold out a bit longer for me?"

"Go-ahead" meant she did need to ask someone else, after all. Though now that I thought about it, this could just be a matter of safety. It was risky sending students, especially the brand-new ones who would be challenging the Beginner's Dungeon to learn the ropes, to a floor that no one had ever seen before without first confirming it was safe. But did Marino really think somewhere I could solo was dangerous? It was a possibility, but was that truly the whole story?

In the end, I was clueless. All I knew was that I wanted to honor Marino's request.

"Got it. I'll keep this information between the members of this house and Yukine until you've gotten confirmation."

"Thanks. I'll be sure to get it by Saturday when you go to challenge it. Until then, it's a Hanamura household secret, okay?"

—Yukine's Perspective—

There were two people in my mind who were synonymous with defying all common sense—my older sister, and Student Council President Monica. But Takioto nearly eclipsed President Monica. Was he ever going to run out of ways to surprise me?

"Keep heading forward, and if there's a four-way split, you go north, west, west, south, south, south, east, south, east, and then north. If there's a regular two-way fork, you'll have to take a different route, though. I'll put these instructions in a table so you can check that later."

It didn't make any sense. Just how far had he gone to obtain this information? Normally, you'd expect this type of intel to be outright hidden or limited to people willing to pay an exorbitant sum for the privilege of obtaining it, but Takioto had simply laid it all out like it was nothing.

I could tell just from listening that he'd gone to great lengths to gather this knowledge. It must've taken a considerable amount of time for him to plot out the patterns and carefully examine the whole dungeon map. On top of that, he'd looked into ways to further reduce the time it took to run through the dungeon.

Takioto had kept running through the Beginner's Dungeon over and over, heedless of his declining reputation on campus, until he'd conclusively announced the findings of his investigations to us.

But having everything handed to us on a silver platter only made me more uneasy. Even when I asked him why he was so quick to provide us with this information...

"I mean, I'm letting you all in on it because I can trust you."

...Takioto gave a flippant response to my question, a huge grin on his face.

Miss Marino had told us not to disclose the secrets of the Beginner's Dungeon, but who in the world would I give this up to after Kousuke had worked so hard to get it? How on earth could I do that when I was indebted to the fruits of his labor?

Ludie and Claris must've felt the same. With Miss Hatsumi... I couldn't really get a good read on her, but given how much concern she had for Takioto, she wasn't going to do anything to his detriment. Though, there was always the chance Takioto had disclosed these secrets to her himself.

After we finished the eleventh layer, Kousuke seemed truly pleased as he looked on at everyone celebrating the skills they'd each obtained. As if their joy was his own.

This look of his after one of us accomplished something never changed, even when Claris or I bested him in a sparring match. Kousuke would look frustrated and disappointed, sure, but above all, he seemed happy to see Claris and me grow stronger.

I sighed, casting a sidelong glance at Ludie, who was watching Takioto soberly going over how his sparring partner had gotten the best of him.

It seemed like something was weighing on Ludie's mind as of late.

I was still in good shape. There were things I could still teach Kousuke regarding melee combat. Ludie, however, had nothing she could give him. On top of that, her very existence was behind most of the criticism students were levying against Takioto. I couldn't blame Ludie for loathing her fan club.

The LLL boys tried to justify themselves by claiming Takioto was "inconveniencing Princess Ludivine by being friendly with her, while refusing to acknowledge the trouble he was causing her." Students outside of the conflict probably found it pretty funny that LLL didn't get that you could say the same about them.

But for Ludie and Takioto, the students at the center of the conflict, this was no laughing matter. It must have been intolerable. That's what I'd expect, at least.

He and Claris restarted their mock battle while Ludie watched on, exhaustion faintly showing on her face. Nanami passed her something to drink.

"Takioto's the victim here, but he isn't fighting back. So Ludie's been worrying about him all on her own."

I decided I would back her up. Nanami, who also understood this, came to Ludie's side as well. And...

"It's okay. I'm watching over her, too."

...the faint presence I had sensed approaching in fact belonged to Miss Hatsumi. She stopped next to me and stared at Takioto and the others, her eyes drooping ever so slightly... Or at least, they seemed to be.

"Thank you, Miss Hatsumi."

Replying with a strained smile, she then turned toward me and stared hard with her robotic eyes.

"Kousuke thinks very highly of you, Yukine. He even said that surpassing you might be his ultimate end goal."

It was a strange thing to hear. Why exactly did he hold me in such high esteem?

I'd asked him this once before. If his goal was to become the strongest of all, then who was going to be his biggest hurdle to overcome?

"Someone stopping me from being the strongest? Well, among the other first-years, there's Ludie, for starters. But the biggest obstacles would have to be President Monica Mercedes von Mobius and you, Yukine. Besides

the other students, there's one crazy, ultimate weapon–level person out there, but... Oh, now that I think about it, there's also a guy in my class who I expect to turn into a real monster."

His thoughts on President Monica made sense. She was practically on a whole other plane of existence than everyone else. She'd grow to be a magic-user capable of rivaling Marino Hanamura.

But how was he able to rank me alongside her? Why did he overestimate my capabilities like my sister had?

Whenever I insisted that I wasn't anything special, Takioto refused to hear it. At this point, he practically idolized me. When we'd argue back and forth about it, my sister's face would abruptly spring to mind. Until now, she'd been the only person to think so highly of me.

Other people had told me I was talented, that was true. But they never went so far as to say I could become more powerful than anyone else. Only my sister and Takioto said that.

"Kousuke's impossible to comprehend. There's a mysterious persuasiveness to what he says. He makes groundless arguments rooted in emotion seem reliable."

He did indeed have mysterious powers of persuasion. There were times he'd make claims that seemed impossible to verify without cultivating many years of life experience. I imagine this was a result of his upbringing and the difficult life he'd led.

There were other times he would spout the wildest things I had ever heard, only to discover them to be true. Like with the hidden layer in the Beginner's Dungeon.

Part of his persuasiveness stemmed from how his words reflected his actions. Everything he did ultimately ended up being the correct choice.

Conversely, an outsider who'd never interacted with him before was bound to take his claims as baseless, unconvincing nonsense.

"Kousuke even said that surpassing you might be his ultimate end goal. And he's aiming to be the strongest of all."

Miss Hatsumi repeated herself once more.

"That's why I'm watching you."

Faced with her robot-like eyes boring into me, I involuntarily averted my gaze.

Suddenly, my sister's words came to mind.

You can become number one, Yukine.

Words that were like a magic charm pushing me forward but also like a weight dragging me down.

"...I don't know if I'll be able to meet your expectations, but I'll be diligent to keep improving myself."

Takioto was going to a different dungeon with Nanami the next day. He was sure to keep on growing at a tremendous rate.

For once, the dungeon we were heading for was actually located on the map. It was, however, listed as "ruins" instead of a "dungeon." Nothing really stood out about the area at a glance, and since you needed to go through a privately owned section of woods to get there, not many people visited.

I could sort of guess why it hadn't been labeled as a dungeon. The requirements to get in were downright merciless.

"This seems to be the place."

Nanami said, putting away the map.

"This is it, huh......?"

It looked like any other cave.

I tried peeking inside, but without any light, I couldn't make out anything in its depths.

"Is there really a dungeon in this place? And forgive my asking, but did you actually find written materials claiming that was the case? There isn't a 'Du' symbol—the mark that indicates the presence of a dungeon—on the map, either."

Nanami had an excessively suspicious look in her eyes.

"I'm telling you, that's what I saw. The document said it's actually a dungeon."

That was what I told her, but of course, I hadn't actually seen anything like that. I'd made up a random lie on the spot as cover, so it wasn't surprising that she was skeptical. The documents outlining the dungeon do actually exist, though. You have to trade in a number of magic stones at a used bookstore somewhere to get them. But this was just a conversation event in-game, so I hadn't been able to go off the visuals to find the shop in this world.

I'd wondered if Iori had gotten his hands on it and had messaged him about it, but alas, it appeared he hadn't found the used book-store, either. That place also sold information about dungeons the developers added in later content updates as well, so I very much wanted him to find it and learn where everything was. Even without those materials, however, I could manage to locate the dungeons myself by comparing my memory of the game with my map, so at least I wasn't completely stuck.

I intensified the mana flowing through my stole and went into the hole.

It was just wide enough to fit a line of four people across. Nanami and I both used Light as we advanced deeper and deeper inside. Then, after we'd headed about 250 feet in, we came to an open space.

"What do you think those are?"

Nanami pointed at three statues inside the open cavern, each depicting a woman holding a sword and staff. The three sculptures were arranged in a triangle, and between them sat three T-shaped pedestals. Each of the female statues hoisted its sword up high in its right hand, while the staff in its left hand was held against its chest.

I immediately went over to the pedestals. Nanami seemed interested in the statues and circled around one to get a closer look.

On top of each pedestal was a triangular cavity, where I surmised we needed to offer up the goods. The area around these devices featured more of the script I couldn't really understand, and while there were a few heroines who could, including Nanami, I already knew what it said.

When Nanami finished inspecting the statues and came over to me, she read the ancient text written around the pedestals.

"'Thou must offer three of the final shields that protect a warrior maiden's body,' is what it says, I think?"

Nanami turned around and stared at the stone statue.

"A final shield...? What could that possibly mean? And three of them, at that... Do you think we just need to present three shields specially made for women?"

I could understand why Nanami would interpret things this way. Anyone who wrote this place off as nothing more than ruins would have the same misunderstanding.

Even in a normal game, if a player heard "Thou must offer three of the final shields that protect a warrior maiden's body," they'd probably imagine armor forged by a goddess or the shield of a hero. And if this were the real world, all the more so.

But for an eroge like *Magical★Explorer*, that interpretation didn't cut it.

"Ummm, welp. I really don't want to say this, but... According to the document I read... The shield protecting a body means clothing... Makes sense, right? So by 'final' they mean..."

"......"

Nanami sent a scowl in my direction, appearing to surmise what I was getting at. I couldn't help feeling an urge to flee. Still, I had to say it.

"Um, it's, well...a woman's...y'know. The last piece of clothing you take off when undressing, that's what we need to offer here... Of course, I didn't think this up, no ma'am. I would never think up anything like this, not me. The document said to do this. That by offering three pairs of panties—used pairs, mind you... We can move forward."

A frigid mood descended on the area.

Nanami was expressionless. Her blank visage only compounded the disgust and anger she was sending my way, and I was just about ready to piss myself in terror. She wasn't even blinking; she just kept her unending stare locked on me.

Oh, I got it. She wasn't directing her glare at *me*. She was glaring at the dungeon, right? A nebulous feeling of guilt welled up inside me when I considered that a fellow eroge enjoyer had created this mechanism.

"No, wait, you've got it all wrong. You gotta believe me!"

Actually, nothing was incorrect. If anything, I'd have gladly wished for such an offering myself under different circumstances. It wasn't even my fault things were like this, really, yet for some reason, I was racked with a strange sense of shame. Pressured by this feeling, I soon found myself prostrated on the ground, begging Nanami's forgiveness.

I knew this was how things would go no matter who I came with, which is why I hadn't even wanted to clear this dungeon in real life!

When I'd first discovered how to unlock the dungeon while playing the game, I was so moved by the sinfulness, the profundity, the practicality of it all that I couldn't help but bow my head in admiration.

A heroine would immediately reject any request for her underwear. Though now that I thought about it, I couldn't say that definitively for every eroge heroine. In some cases, they weren't wearing any to begin with! Typically, though, they'd refuse outright. That's why concocting a scenario in which the only way forward was forcing the heroines to hand over their panties was absolutely supreme eroge design. My first playthrough, I'd immediately brought my favorite party members to plunge into this dungeon. I mean, who wouldn't?

Then, when the words "Who's panties will you offer?" and a selection of the heroines in your party showed up on the screen, how was anyone supposed to stop their mouse hand from trembling with anticipation?

Depending on which heroine the player chooses, they are treated to an icy cold glare and rewarded with titillating insults of "idiot," "pervert," and the like. Then she gives the player a warning: "If nothing ends up happening, you know what's coming, right?" Once they offer up the panties, freshly removed in a fit of indignant embarrassment, the game really does advance forward. It sure does work like a charm, yessiree. It skips right to the next screen.

Oh, how many times had I reloaded my save to see each character's dialogue...?!

That wasn't all, either; the game slips in special exchanges based on which characters you bring to the dungeon with you. With the help of the gentlemen tasked with editing the game wiki, I'd tried out every pattern possible. It was truly a riveting moment of the game.

Even more surprising was that with heroines added in later patches, the game not only shows them taking off their panties for this scene, but also gives them brand-new dialogue patterns for the player to enjoy.

I'd thought it was masterful.

Moooooore like disasterful.

Whoever thought this up was a hopeless buffoon. How the hell are you supposed to go up to a woman and ask her to give you her used panties? Who could even ask that—are you insane? Sure, you could forgive this idiotic little scenario in an eroge, but in real life, it was nothing but god-awful, batshit-crazy design. The guy who thought this up must have had his brain scrambled with smut. If they needed to offer something to the dungeon, there were plenty of more sensible options! Swords, gems, anything! The strangest point of all this, however, was the stipulation that the panties needed to be *used* instead of new. That was a whole other level of perverted. We could have bought brand-new panties at the Academy co-op or a convenience store or something. It would have been so much easier.

"...Well, there you have it. It's the dungeon's fault."

Even while I gave her any and all sorts of explanations I could come up with, I stayed bowing on the floor, daunted by the pressure I felt from Nanami.

The maid breathed a small sigh. Then she told me to stand up and took my hand.

"My apologies. I know this is not your fault, Master, but I couldn't hold back my disgust."

At these words, I raised my head. Nanami looked almost like an angel, gently smiling down at me. Wait, she actually *was* an angel.

"I have no problem with offering up my own pair... However."

"However?"

"Is there any chance that...offering up your own underwear...would also suffice?"

Excuse me?

"Master has somewhat androgynous facial features, so if we swap out your eyes, ears, nose, and mouth, plus fix your hair, you'd be quite the pretty young boy."

"Isn't that basically turning me into someone else? If you swap out my eyes, ears, nose, and mouth, there's basically none of my own features left."

"Please, there is no need to fear. I will offer up my own as well with you. The thought of offering my panties to anyone besides you is gruesomely displeasing; even now, I can feel an urge growing inside me to completely annihilate this planet, but I will restrain myself to releasing only seventy percent of my full power."

"So you're cool with giving them to me, then... Still. Seventy percent of full power seems like it'd leave the world in rough shape."

"Shall we take them off, then?"

"Wait, it's just, that other condition, see... About being from 'warrior maidens...'"

"Have you tried using your own?"

"Well, no, I haven't..."

"Face that way and take off your underwear, then. I'll remove mine, too. When I lift up my skirt, I'll let you know, so be sure to turn around quick and sneak a peek, okay?"

"Is this some type of exhibitionist thing?"

I was absolutely, positively, definitely not going to look.

"Eek."

She did realize that barely three seconds had passed since I turned around, right? No way was I peeking.

I heaved a sigh. How had things ended up like this?

The one consolation was that Nanami wouldn't peek over at me, like Sis and Ms. Ruija. With an odd feeling of dissatisfaction coming over me, I took off my boxers and put my pants back on, underwear-free. I then called out to Nanami and put them on one of the pedestals.

Following my lead, Nanami placed her panties on another device. They were white.

There was an immediate response.

A bright light emanated from one of the statues, then immediately formed a single beam that extended from the tip of the sword to spotlight the pedestal and the panties.

"Y-you've gotta be kidding."

The two glimmering pairs of underwear on the pedestal slowly began to float up into the air, gradually glowing brighter still.

If the shimmering items had been anything else, it would've made for a fantastic sight.

Nanami's panties glimmered and glimmered, before finally dissolving into pure light.

Meanwhile, my boxers glimmered and glimmered before finally... catching on fire.

"Whaaaaaaaaaat?"

They fluttered back down to the ground. The flames, however, remained.

An orb of water flew out from beside me as I paced helter-skelter. Nanami had used water magic on my behalf. The ball hit my flaming shorts. Though it succeeded in dousing the blaze, my underwear now had a huge hole in a spot that needed covering.

It didn't look like I'd ever be using this pair again.

"......"

The panties-less maid was at a loss for words. She must have been shaken up.

"You all right, Nanami?"

"Well, my undergarments returned to the pedestal, and I always carry a full change of clothes with me, so I'm fine… Wh-what about you, Master?"

She glanced at me uneasily. I couldn't say if it was a reaction to my boxers going up in flames, or from the refreshing sensation of going commando, but I was strangely at peace.

"It's okay, I'm fine. And, hmm, how can I describe it? At this point, it feels like no matter what else happens, I'd just shrug it off with a smile."

"Uh-oh. That event was so shocking, it transformed you into a bodhisattva."

Anyway…

"So *this* is what I was asking you to do. I see; I'll make sure anyone who comes to clear this dungeon with me brings another pair of panties with them."

Though it took going commando to do it, I'd learned something. I'd make sure anyone who came with me to this place brought another change of underwear. That settled it.

"Um, well. D-do you have a change of clothes, Master…?

"Nah, I didn't think things through, so I didn't bring any. But I'm pretty sure I have something that'll do the trick…"

I rummaged through my bag. Deep in the bottom, I caught a glimpse of some sort of black string…… *String?*

"What's this?"

In the center of the string was a thin piece of fabric. I knew what this was. It was the sacred piece of fabric that protected the most precious part of a person's body. Panties. Sexy black panties that looked *very* familiar. The panties I'd accidentally gotten ahold of when Claris was busy moving in with the Hanamura's.

"W-wait! I promise it's n-not what you think! These aren't mine!"

"……Then whose are they, exactly?"

"Th-they're Claris's! Definitely, one hundred percent not mine!"

"…Then why exactly do you have a pair of her panties in your possession?"

"Gaaaaaaaaaaaah!"

I hadn't tried to steal them on purpose. Absolutely not.

Of course, panties were a sublime commodity, on par with any precious gem, and since this pair belonged to a gorgeous elf woman, I really couldn't help thinking that I would've loved to get my hands on them, no matter how enormous a price they'd command.

Nevertheless, gentlemen like ourselves don't actually wish to become criminals. If anything, we loathe those who engage in illegal acts.

Eroge and reality were two separate worlds. That was precisely why I subscribed to "YES loli, NO touch," and believed YES, loli characters (over the age of eighteen) in eroge, and YES, self-control.

Buuuuut, if I blurted all of that out, people would only treat me like even more of a deranged pervert. So naturally, I pushed through by saying I'd missed the chance to give the panties back to Claris and avoided mentioning anything else.

The problem was, it was unclear to me how Nanami felt about my explanation.

Afterward, I fervently pleaded for us to go straight back home. Despite being tormented by a disquieting sensation in my nether regions with each step I took, I managed to make it back to the house. Immediately donning a fresh pair of underwear, I began racking my brain about who I should invite to come back to the dungeon with me.

Personally, I wanted to invite Yukine, Ludie, and Claris. They were all my usual sparring partners, and I understood how each of them moved in combat, so it would be easy to coordinate with them.

Unfortunately, the biggest problem with this dungeon was the idiotic puzzle design that someone with lewd thoughts streaming out of both ears had come up with.

What was I going to do about the panties? This was likely the most I'd agonized over a situation in my entire life. Did I know anyone who would shrug off a request to offer up their used smallclothes to me?

In that light, I was definitely bringing Nanami, because she'd already experienced it for herself. I'd always wanted to have her come with me because of her technical abilities, so adding her to my party was a no-brainer. The problem was the other members besides her.

Would Ludie or Yukine offer up their underwear? If it was only the panties I had to worry about, then I always had the option of asking Ms. IOU; she seemed like she'd give them up if I ordered her.

The trick was that if I asked her to "give me your used panties," it would come off like a debt collector asking for them in exchange for money, an absurd eroge-like situation. Though, I guess this *was* an eroge world, in the end.

I'd totally be up for trying this if a game gave me the opportunity. In real life, however, I didn't want to do something so cruel to the poor woman. Though if I truly ran out of alternatives, I'll admit there was a non-zero chance that I'd bow down and beg her for them.

That reminded me—sometimes adult magazines came with panties as a special bonus. Would those work? This one publication even included a perfumed pair of undergarments with their issues.

Probably not. I bet they'd get burned to a crisp, too.

"Hey, Nanami. What do you think I should do? Prostrate in front of them?"

"...First, I believe it would be best to verify everyone's schedules. For those who can join you, you could get down on your hands and knees and beg for mercy.

"That really is the only option, isn't it...?"

Begging on the floor seemed set in stone.

I immediately took out my Tsukuyomi Traveler to text a few people.

Standing before me were Ludie, Yukine, Nanami, and Sis. Claris, Marino, and Ms. Ruija had all been busy and couldn't make it. But now that I thought about it, Ms. Ruija and Marino said they were tied up with work, so it was weird that Sis was here...... Should she really have come along?

After all my potential party members gathered around the statues of the three warrior maidens, I immediately kissed the ground with my forehead and began begging them for their underwear. Nanami was ready to prostrate herself right alongside me, but I politely refused her offer.

I'd actually planned on mentioning the purpose of this trip when I first texted them, but I chickened out. Try as I might, I couldn't bring the subject up.

It was not until we arrived at the dungeon entrance that I found the strength to tell them. A small part of me hoped that they'd respond with something like, "Well, we've come all this way, and it sounds unbelievable, but I'll hand them over."

My pleas sounded like both an excuse and repentance. As my explanation reached its climax, and I was on the verge of declaring that I would do anything they asked as long as they gave me the panties they were wearing, I felt a tap on my shoulder.

"Pick your head up, Takioto."

Those kind words came from Yukine. Ludie wore a conflicted look, while Sis was gazing my way with her usual blank expression, pacing aimlessly around the warrior maiden statues. I had no clue what Nanami was thinking, but she stood at my side.

Yukine took my hand and helped me up.

In spite of the subtle pinkish flush on her face, she smiled cheerfully.

"I know we haven't been acquainted for very long. But I know you well enough to tell that you're not someone who'd lie about this stuff... So."

She was embarrassed after all. Normally, Yukine would fix her pretty eyes on mine when we spoke; today, however, not only was she refusing to look me in the eye, but she was also restlessly swaying her body back and forth. The situation was really getting to her.

"Y-Yukine..."

She went to say something and opened her mouth slightly before ultimately staying silent, hanging her head down while her face burned crimson from ear to ear. Then she ran a hand through her perfectly kept hair. When at last she found the resolve to speak, the feeble voice that accompanied her was unlike any I could have ever imagined coming from the Yukine I knew.

"So, well, um... It's a bit embarrassing, but if my unsightly pair will do the trick, um... Please use them."

She followed up with a "Don't look at me," before she turned her back to me in an attempt to conceal her flushed face. Her ears were still beet red, though, so she didn't really hide much of anything.

Now it was safe to say the long-awaited moment had arrived. Right here, right now, I was announcing the inauguration of YYY. "Yukine, Yearning for Yukine" could work. Yukine was like a goddess, so it'd end up meaning "Yukine, Yearning for the Goddess," which I thought had a nice ring to it. "Yes, Yes, Yukine" could work, too. That would be easier to use when it came time to expand the fan club overseas.

"Kousuke."

As I considered how to market the fan club across the globe, Ludie also appeared to make up her mind, then stared at me.

"I also don't think you're someone who would tell a weird joke in this sort of situation. So, it's embarrassing for me, too, but...," Ludie then continued. "Besides, you're always the one helping me. I want to be there for you, too. If something comes up, I want you to come to me about it. Like you did this time."

She averted her gaze.

"Still, this truly is embarrassing... But if it's to help you out, Kousuke... I'd give you as many of my panties as you need."

Once Ludie finished saying her piece, she hung her head, as though embarrassed that what she'd just said had actually came out of her mouth. A moment later, she turned her back from me.

I was so very, very happy. Honestly, I figured Ludie was going to hurl insults at me. Though we were relatively close with each other, I would have had no room to complain if she'd slammed a letter denouncing our friendship right in my face the moment I asked her to fork over her panties.

".......Thank you, Ludie."

She acknowledged me quietly, her back still turned away from me.

"Kousuke."

Next it was Sis's turn. As soon as I responded, she handed something to me. Curious as to what it was, I unfurled the fabric.

It was an article of clothing that covered one's most important parts, pink garnished with a black lace flair. The fabric that covered the rear was thin enough that I could see my hand through it. It would leave little to the imagination when you put it on.

These were a pair of sexy pink and black panties.

What......?

I was losing it. Calm down. Take a deep breath. These were just what she brought to change into, right? She was just having me check them. Why, it was important to have someone knowledgeable confirm that they were acceptable.

Now wait just a minute here. Even if she were getting me to check them, she wouldn't need to actually hand them off to me, right? Heck, did she even need to show them to me at all? Was she mistaking me for an authority on this dungeon or something? *Uhhh?*

Maybe she'd gotten changed? But there definitely hadn't been enough time for that. Though I hoped that my mind was simply playing tricks on me, the panties seemed faintly warm. *Umm...*

"S-Sis? I—I get it, right? These are the panties you brought to change into, yeah…?"

"I can really feel the cool breeze. It's refreshing."

"Freshly picked, got it! Hurry up and change into your spare pair!"

I returned Sis's panties back to her and headed back to the entrance of the cave like a gentleman. Nevertheless.

To be honest, I *really* wanted to watch them undress. Sneak a peek, if possible. But I couldn't justify that when those three were fighting back their embarrassment…er, when those *two* were fighting back their embarrassment to hand me their panties. It would be unforgivable to look.

Well then, what was I supposed to do?

It was time for the power of imagination. This level of fantasizing was nothing for someone who had over a hundred different eroge titles under his belt…

"Master."

I was totally immersed in my vision, imagining Ludie and Yukine reaching for their clothes. Just then, I heard someone call out from behind me. When I turned around, I found Nanami standing there to greet me.

For some reason, she was bowing apologetically.

"I'm terribly sorry. Originally, I was supposed to supply the panties myself. This was my big chance to demonstrate my position as your most loyal retainer, but I've been outdone……!"

She didn't need to do that. Anyway, why was she getting upset with me?

"Well, we can put that aside for a moment. You see, Master, I am very disappointed."

"What's there to be disappointed about…?"

"That my scheme to make you cross-dress and offer up your panties in the hopes they might be miraculously mistaken for a girl's pair ♪ came crashing down. It was still too early to throw in the towel."

"It failed because you were trying to back me into a corner. Would it kill you to considering my feelings here?"

Like hell I was doing any cross-dressing. Go make some eroge protagonist deal with that nonsense. But why was she so hyped about the idea?"

"Drat, and I had planned on ultimately squishing your face into my chest so I could pat your head and console you afterward, too. What a shame."

What an attractive proposition. If I pretended to get hit with some mental strain right now, would she still do that for me? Hold on, that was all under the premise that my cross-dressing would end up failing, though.

"With that in mind, here…"

She held something out for me. It was a piece of fabric with light blue and white stripes.

Nanami wouldn't be the type to pass me a handkerchief in a moment like this. It didn't even look like a handkerchief in the first place, what with the adorable little ribbon on it. No, it took me all of a second to figure out what this item was.

"L-look, I don't need to use yours, okay?" I protested, but Nanami ignored that and got up right in front of me to place the "gift" in my breast pocket. She patted my pocket in smug satisfaction before sliding back away from me.

Though I immediately attempted to return the pair of striped panties to her, she refused to accept them.

"No. I insist on showing you my sincerity. That's all."

"I—I get it, I get it. You've definitely made that clear. S-so I don't need these, okay? Hell, what am I even supposed to do with these anyway?!"

At my reply, Nanami drew within a hair's breadth of me and softly whispered into my ear.

"You're still holding on to Miss Claris's pair, aren't you?"

I gulped.

Why did she know that?

I needed to say something to explain myself, but the words wouldn't come… I frantically considered how I needed to handle the situation. But Nanami's next statement proved faster than mine.

"You wanted them, did you not? Mine are especially high-quality. Put them on your head and it'll raise your defense."

"I'm not looking for high defense stats from a pair of underwear. And to be honest, the idea of wearing them on my head never even crossed my mind. I mean, I'd just put them on like a normal person. Actually, no, wait, imagining that is equally awful."

"In that case, think of them as a protective charm and carry them with you. Another way of putting it, I suppose, is that I would be offended if I were the only one not to give you a pair. That and…I would feel like I lost, somehow."

There weren't really any winners or losers with stuff like this…

Saying this, Nanami backed away from me with satisfaction and headed off into the cave.

Carefully putting her panties away, I hurried after her.

The others had just finished getting ready and were on their way to call us back into the cave. I stood close to the warrior maiden statues, consciously avoiding any direct looks at Yukine and the others while I was hiding Nanami's undergarments. Everyone else began to move into their positions.

The three giving up their panties each stood before a pedestal and began preparing their offerings.

They each held a neatly folded pair of underwear. Ludie and Yukine were covering their offerings with both hands and still looked a little pink as they threw occasional glances my way.

Sis, on the other hand, was clearly the odd one out. She was holding her panties out wide, tightly stretching them open by the top seam. Her pose was so dignified that it almost looked like she was accepting some sort of award. The real question was why she was being so brazen about this in the first place.

"Okay, let's start."

At Sis's insistence, the three women placed their panties on the pedestals.

Just like what had happened with my boxers, the devices responded immediately.

A bright glow emanated from the statues, which then abruptly coalesced into a single beam of light that extended from the tip of the sword to spotlight the pedestal and the panties.

When the beam faded, the glimmering undergarments slowly floated up into the air from the pedestals. Yukine had folded up her panties so nicely, but now they were slowly beginning to unfurl in the light. The girl had been so hesitant to show her underwear to anyone else that this may as well have been her public execution.

Her panties were blue, with a snowflake design woven into the fabric. They matched perfectly with the snow character in her name. I bet just a glimpse of her wearing those babies would knock me unconscious for a week.

Like Yukine's, Ludie's ivory undergarments had opened up for all to see. The pure whiteness of her undergarments only further instilled the impression of chastity and nobility she gave off. Yet the pair floating in the air in front of me were far more risqué than I would've expected. While they were indeed virtuous, there was something just slightly off-kilter about them. This pair's daring and aggressive edge made my heart skip a beat.

Sis's panties, which had been etched into my memory moments prior, didn't open up at all. They'd been unreservedly spread wide open right from the start.

Just then, I realized that there were eyes on me.

Ludie and Yukine were staring, begging me to look away.

I felt like I was going to cough up blood...

Moving like a machine that hadn't been oiled in a century, I used both hands to laboriously turn my face away from my view of paradise. Then, heart weeping in my chest, I etched the sight of these three treasures into the depths of my memory.

It was about a minute later when Nanami gave me permission to lift my head back up.

When I opened my eyes, I was greeted with serious expressions from Nanami, Ludie, and Yukine, a complete departure from how they'd looked moments before. Meanwhile, Sis seemed the same as ever.

A magic circle had appeared in the middle of the three pedestals.

I took a deep breath and filled my stole with mana before making two, then three practice swings. Yukine produced her naginata, Ludie and Sis their staffs, Nanami her bow and short sword, and they each began to prepare themselves for combat.

I, too, retrieved my katana from my bag. After confirming with everyone that they were ready to go, I took a step inside the circle.

When hearing the word *dungeon*, I imagine the first word that comes to mind for most people is *traps*.

A great many players of roguelikes or other similar games, myself included, have probably enjoyed several lifetimes' worth of these devices' painful blessings before.

Literally, several lives' worth.

Landmines exploding at your feet, switches that release monsters, pitfalls that bottom out into the nest of a creature.

Now, this is merely my personal impression, but it seems that the most unfair ways to die in these games usually involved traps. I absolutely hated when I'd be tearing my way through a dungeon, only to have a trap immediately push me to the brink of death. I truly, truly *loathed* them.

Up until I was in high school.

In the world of eroge and other pretty girl–focused games—recently with manga and anime as well—these sorts of traps are at their best. The great thing about them is that they revolve around snagging the heroines in some dubious liquid or tentacle-like appendages, or forcing them into lewd poses, or in extreme cases, hiding enemies in a pitfall who have attacks that will only dissolve a character's clothing—situations that make it impossible to keep a level head.

Magical★Explorer is no exception. Like any other eroge, when the characters are caught in a trap, your dungeon crawl will immediately grind to a halt to show you a CG of the event. That way, you can admire the scene and sear it into your brain.

But unfortunately, this was real life. I couldn't do anything like that. Though, when I'd rescued Ludie, such a trap provided me with a lovely opportunity.

Now, the latest dungeon we'd at last gained access to, the Gloomy Ruins, is filled with traps. You can't clear this dungeon without installing a retailer-exclusive bonus patch, and it isn't exactly required to build the strongest possible character, so there are likely many gentlemen who skip it entirely.

Nevertheless, there are several items hidden in its depths that make clearing other dungeons down the line much easier in a first-time playthrough. One of them I wanted to get my hands on so badly that I had come here fully prepared to be looked at like a pervert to get it. That was why…

"I need to snag that item at all costs…"

I gave a small sigh as I punched the wrappings off a mummy with my Third Hand. The mummy fell to the ground, and its body gradually dissipated into magic particles and a magic stone.

Now, what sort of monster is a mummy exactly? They are corpses, dried out like beef jerky and wrapped up in bandages from head to toe, save for a portion of their face. These sorts of undead, which wouldn't be out of place in an Egyptian pyramid, are often used as a monster in other fantasy games.

The first word that came to mind as I looked at them was *disgusting*. The mummy's face, slightly blackened and lacking any vitality, takes a mental toll on you.

Fighting these undead-type monsters in later dungeons was going to be annoying. Since the mummies were all dried out, they didn't smell too bad. But zombies are a different story. Their rotten bodies reek so intensely that even the game characters comment about the stench being unbearable. Honestly, I didn't want to fight them at all. They show up in a required dungeon down the line, though, so it was all but guaranteed I'd end up seeing them.

We were only fighting humanoid mummies at the moment, but later on in this dungeon, and in later dungeons, animal-shaped mummies would appear, too. Goat mummies, gazelle mummies, lion mummies, and more. Fortunately, none of the monsters that showed up in this dungeon were very strong, so I didn't need to worry about them too much.

As I picked up the magic stone, Nanami came over to me.

"That was a wonderful battle, Master."

"Nah, couldn't have done it without you backing me up. Find Traps is saving our hides, too."

Nanami's backline support with her bow was actually helping me out a lot, and sometimes she would defeat an enemy before I could get in melee range.

"I am simply glad what little power I have is proving beneficial. That said, I do not have much confidence in my Find Traps skill, so I caution against relying on it too heavily...," Nanami said, looking apologetic. But based on her performance in the game, her detection rate was out of this world.

In *Magical★Explorer*, skills that detect traps have levels; the higher the level, the easier it is to discover them.

While Nanami can raise her Find Traps level easily, it starts at level zero. Meanwhile, Katarina naturally has a certain number of levels in her detection skills because her main class has thief skills. Additionally, she has relatively high levels in both Disarm Trap, which is used to negate traps on treasure chests, and Unlock, which you can use to pick the locks on treasure chests.

Initially, I'd estimated that Nanami had an 80 to 90 percent chance of detecting traps. But thus far, she'd boasted a 100 percent detection rate on up to the third layer of the dungeon, so it was possible that the Maid-Knight Servant Heaven Form was equipped with another ability of some kind. Though, there was always the chance that she had actually missed some, and we'd just been lucky enough to avoid stepping on them.

Now, while avoiding these devices was a good thing, it was also devastatingly disappointing.

We weren't getting caught in anything.

I was missing the chance of seeing Ludie or Yukine forced into an erotic situation and explaining it all away with a helpless Find Traps slipup.

If they were going to get ensnared in a trap, I would've preferred it happen in one here in the Gloomy Ruins, since they didn't cause any physical harm.

Alas, it seemed that, too, would never come to pass. Given that Nanami had already detected a lot of traps at this point, her skill level had to be going up with it. The dungeon was filled with nothing but low-grade traps, so it was fair to say it was designed to serve as an introduction to that mechanic.

It seemed the fighting on the opposite end had also wrapped up. Ludie and Yukine came over to us.

"Feels like overkill with us all here."

Yukine smiled ironically as she spoke.

She was spot-on. The monsters in here didn't even hold up to what appeared on the twelfth layer of the Tsukuyomi Magic Academy Dungeon. As was often the case with pre-order bonus or limited-edition bonus content, this place was a low-level dungeon that players could clear on their first playthrough. For Yukine, who had likely cleared down to the fiftieth layer of the Tsukuyomi Dungeon, or Sis, who had graduated and fully cleared sixty layers, the monsters here were probably putting them to sleep.

In fact, Yukine and Sis were intentionally hanging back and holding off from fighting to help Ludie, Nanami, and me gain experience. But even with a party of three, nothing up until now had put us in danger.

"Not another forked path…," Ludie grumbled, looking fed up as she came near.

There were two paths before us. We had already reached several dead ends by this point, and Ludie seemed a little tired. It would be a good idea to take a break once we got to the next layer.

"Which way shall we go?"

I had no way of answering Nanami's question. The layout of this dungeon changed every time you entered, so I was clueless.

"Doesn't matter either way, really… Let's go right, then." Nobody else showed any indication of preferring one way over the other, so I simply picked a path at random to go down. It became clear shortly after starting down the path that I had made the correct choice. In front of us were the stairs leading down to the lower layer.

"*Hngh… Haah, haah…,*" Ludie panted after I stopped sending her my mana. Then she leaned up against me as she got her breathing under control. Seeing her sweat-soaked hair stuck to her cheeks and forehead and the glassy look in her eyes troubled me. No, not "troubled." Past progressive: They *were* troubling me.

Just then, I released my grip on Ludie's warm, slightly damp hand. When I did, a small gasp escaped her lips.

All right, was there something up with my Donation Magic? According to Claris, the sensation of getting magic from me was like receiving a strange massage, but when she did the same for me, it didn't feel anything like that. If this was in some game, I'd be fine with it, but having things get like this in real life was problematic. Especially when I had to donate mana right before a battle.

It didn't seem like ruminating on it would bring me to an answer, so I decided to put it aside for now. I still had another question:

Why were Sis and Nanami standing side by side and gazing longingly this way?

Angels like Nanami needed mana just to move, so I could sort of see why she would want some from me. I had tested out donating mana to her previously, and she'd expended a bit in combat, so it wouldn't be strange to top her off.

But why was Sis lined up with her, exactly? She'd barely used any magic at all.

I wanted her to look at Yukine. She was giving her body the rest it needed and... Wait, what was with that tormented expression Sis was giving Ludie...? M-must be my imagination.

After Sis and Nanami made me promise I would use Donation Magic on them when we got back to the house, we continued on.

From there, we descended through a number of layers until finally arriving at the sixth floor. The encounters here weren't much different from the ones on the previous layers, save for the fact that Yukine was now participating in combat.

She seemed to have grown antsy watching on the sidelines and was now using her magic with excessive enthusiasm.

I slammed into a Sand Golem, freshly drenched in Yukine's Water Ball, and it broke apart. While I stared vacantly at the creature as it dissolved into magic particles and a magic stone, a voice came from behind me.

"Why are you always pushing yourself so hard, Takioto?"

The voice belonged to Yukine. I got the feeling we had discussed this before at some point...

"Because I want to become the strongest of all...?"

Though, I didn't plan on talking about my real objective.

"Aren't you going a bit too hard? You also need to rest, you know."

It was probably because I was challenging dungeons almost every day. Now that I thought about it, I didn't see anyone else run them as much as I did. That said, I still thought Yukine's own daily training regimen was equal, if not superior, to my own.

"No, if I'm really going to become that strong, I need to put in the effort now to get there."

The person who I'd sworn to overcome, Iori Hijiri, was unmistakably overpowered.

Currently, Iori was focused on his classes and was delving into different dungeons than the ones I was clearing. He'd told me he would try descending into a new dungeon soon. As far as I could tell, he didn't appear to have any information about our current one, the Gloomy Ruins. That didn't surprise me, considering it was bonus content.

Iori's activities were a perfect encapsulation of what a first-time player with no prior knowledge would do in the game at this point.

I was stronger than him right now. There was no doubt about that. However, as the protagonist, he would grow stronger simply as a consequence of his normal progress.

And that progress of his wouldn't stay normal for long.

Going forward, Iori would learn one useful and unique skill after another, overtaking me in strength with his overpowered abilities. To make sure I could stand side by side with his explosive growth... Or rather, I was doing everything in my power right now to make sure I was staying one step ahead of him.

Fortunately, I had access to a wonderful weapon of knowledge, honed by the research of gentlemen like myself. The peculiar, but by no means weak, Kousuke Takioto.

Iori wasn't the only one I needed to surpass, either. I also had the monsters in the Big Three to think about.

I stared at Yukine.

Today she was dressed in navy-blue martial arts *hakama* robes. Her hair was bound in a ponytail and hanging down her back. The exposed nape of her neck was sublime, a feast for the eyes that could sustain me for weeks. She was gorgeous no matter how many times I looked at her, but today, she was especially beautiful.

"Don't you want to get stronger, too, Yukine?"

"I do, but..."

Yukine trailed off, but I gathered what she wanted to say. She still had an inferiority complex toward people more powerful than her, toward her older sister.

"Then let's grow stronger together. We'll invite Ludie with us, and we can charge down through all hundred layers of the Tsukuyomi Academy Dungeon in a snap."

Well, there were actually 101 layers... Oh well, that wasn't important. The one problem with that lay in the dungeon you challenged right after you finished clearing the Tsukuyomi Academy Dungeon. There was a chance I might just leave everything there for Iori to finish.

"*Ha-ha*, what in the world are you talking about? The Tsukuyomi Academy Dungeon tops out at eighty-seven layers," Yukine said, chuckling. *Right, a mere eighty-seven layers, of course.*

"I'm being pretty serious here... So it's impossible for you to come with me after all?"

Suddenly, I considered Yukine's position in this world. She was the lieutenant (vice president) of the Morals Committee. People idolized her, even in-game. She must've already formed another party.

In *MX*, she generally tags along when invited, but now I realized that it'd be normal for her to prioritize her already established party. I couldn't argue with her giving the inexperienced newbie lower priority.

As I was imagining her rejection, she started chuckling.

"No, I wouldn't mind tagging along, as long as my schedule permits."

A strong slap hit my back. Yukine then walked off toward the others. I followed after her swinging ponytail, porcelain nape, and well-shaped butt.

Working through the Sand Golem zones of the seventh, eighth, and ninth layers, we at last arrived on the last level of the dungeon, which held the item I was after. The tenth floor had a fixed layout, unlike the random layouts of the preceding floors. The layout was pretty typical for the final layer of a dungeon—a single path straight to the boss room.

We stopped for a brief moment's rest, got ourselves prepared, and went to challenge the boss.

Appearing before us was a lion mummy.

As their name suggests, these monsters are mummified lions. They look like a morbidly thin female lion that has been painted black.

The speed and severity of its attacks slightly surpassed the Fire Chariot from the Twilight Cavern. But this fight wasn't difficult in the slightest. For starters, the Gloomy Ruins dungeon was around the same level as the Twilight Cavern. The same went for the boss, but this time around, I wasn't going it alone.

I was able to cleanly react to all of its attacks and easily timed my guards with my stole. Right after I blocked two of its blows, Ludie tore into it with Wind Cutter to force it back. I then sent it flying into the wall with a punch, and after Nanami's arrow exploded into it, Ludie finished it off with Storm Hammer for a flawless victory. We'd given it such a sound thrashing, I almost pitied the poor monster.

"...Almost too easy, wasn't it?"

"...Yeah."

It really had been effortless. The only impression the boss left on me was the childish thought that its claws were sort of scary.

I'd made sure to prepare a fire sigil stone for the beast, since all mummy-type enemies shared a weakness to flame, but as it happened, our own fire*power* was too overpowering for it to handle.

Ordinarily, we could've challenged a dungeon a level higher than this. Though actually, my plan after finishing one more dungeon was to challenge another one at about this same level.

We continued onward after Ludie picked up the magic stone from the lion mummy. At the end of the boss room was a single treasure chest. Constructed from wood and iron, the container undoubtedly held the item I was after.

Ludie and Yukine approached the chest with big smiles. Sis and Nanami followed closely behind them.

I tilted my head, thinking for a moment. Now that we were here, I recalled reloading my save a number of times when I went to open this chest. Why exactly had I done that?

Outside of collecting CG scenes, was there any reason for me to reload my save like that?

As I followed after everyone, an image of Ludie, drenched and slimy, suddenly popped into my brain.

"Uh-oh."

I remembered. There was a trap here. It wasn't a trap from the tactical role-playing part of the game, either. No, it was from the romance adventure part.

If memory served, there was a pitfall in front of the treasure chest. It was an event trap, so it activated no matter how high your Find Traps skill was, and the bottom was covered in a slimy, thick liquid that turned you on. And as was often the case with these eroge situations, the aphrodisiac effect only applied to women.

Since the chest was part of an event, Nanami's Find Traps wouldn't function like normal. Ludie and the others hadn't noticed, either.

Was it okay for me to let them keep walking forward unaware?

My head filled with images of Yukine and Ludie, drenched in liquid.

In one sense, I'd get to see the sight I'd eagerly been waiting for if they fell in. Still, was it really okay for me to willfully stay silent despite knowing what would happen?

Suppose they did fall, and I focused my whole body and soul on giving them a good long look, backing up the memory twice over in the recesses of my mind—would I be able to interact with them the same way going forward?

Yeah, no. I couldn't let it happen.

"Ludie, Yukine, don't move!"

At almost the exact instant I said that, it happened. With a rumble, the floor beneath Ludie and Yukine's feet split apart.

I extended my Third and Fourth Hands out to the falling duo. But I couldn't reach them. I was too late. Nonetheless, I jumped into the hole, thinking that there could be some slight chance of saving them.

In midair, I grabbed Ludie in my Third Hand and Yukine in my Fourth, then lifted them up above my head. After that, I braced myself for impact.

There was almost none. Rather than a *splat*, it was more accurate to say I landed with a *squish*.

I had plunged into the infamous liquid. However, there wasn't too much of it, only enough to reach my knees. The liquid also seemed to have absorbed the impact of the fall. I wasn't hurting anywhere. I could drop an egg into this pitfall, and it would probably remain intact.

Since I'd landed on my butt, however, I was pretty soaked.

"Ludie, Yukine, you okay?"

"I-I'm all right."

"Same here…"

As I looked around, I kept the two girls in the air to make sure they didn't get wet. Eventually, I saw what looked like stairs, and after confirming they were free of liquid, I set them down.

Normally, you wouldn't think a trap would use a staircase to help its victims escape, but…… Maybe that was because it was a special, erotic variety?

We met up with Nanami and Sis as they came down to meet us, then all returned back to the area above for the time being. Immediately after ascending the stairs, Sis checked my body.

"I've got a bad feeling about this liquid. Yukine."

Yukine nodded and quickly washed me off with water magic. Meanwhile, Sis sent some poison-curing magic my way.

"Kousuke…," Ludie muttered. As I glanced from her to Yukine, anxiously wielding her water magic, I let out a sigh of relief.

"You two are safe… Thank goodness."

I was truly glad they were all right. If they'd ended up all slimy, I'd have gotten so aroused in spite of my tormented conscience that I might've accidently blasted off into a whole new world beyond.

"I-I'm sorry. I was careless…"

"Sorry. I was sloppy, too."

Both of them expressed remorse, but...

"Please, you don't need to apologize."

In actuality, I was the one to blame. If I had acted sooner, we wouldn't be dealing with this miserable outcome. Besides, I'd wanted to see Ludie and Yukine looking sexy so bad that I'd debated staying silent on purpose.

"Kousuke..."

Ludie was attempting to wipe me off with a towel but stopped abruptly. There, gripping the towel tight in her hands, she looked overcome with emotion. Yukine had also forgot about using her water magic and was staring at me in a daze.

"Master......"

I glanced at the source of the voice to my side. There stood Nanami, who seemed to be chiding herself internally. She gave me a deep bow.

"Allow me to express my deepest apologies."

What's she talking about? I thought.

"I wasn't able to detect the trap."

At this, I shook my head. What, was that it?

"You don't need to apologize. I've been relying on you all day, both for finding traps and helping me fight.

And in regard to this incident... I was cleeeearly the one at fault, no question about it. Sheesh, I really didn't want them looking at me with those eyes. It made me feel even guiltier.

After my party wiped me down the best they could, we moved on. My goal was right before me—the treasure chest. Still reeling from the trap that had sprung earlier, Ludie opened it with great caution. Everyone brought their faces toward mine, and we peered into it together.

Inside were five rings. One inlaid with a red jewel, one inlaid with a blue jewel, one inlaid with a green jewel, and another inlaid with a yellow jewel. Finally, there was one other grungy-looking ring.

The same as in the game. The four jeweled rings each boosted the power of fire, water, wind, and earth elemental skills, respectively. For something you could obtain so early in the game, their abilities...

"...Incredible power."

"I've challenged a bunch of dungeons at this point, but I've never seen anything this strong before."

...were relatively usef... *Huh?* Sis and Yukine had to be joking, right? "You really can sense this amazing power."

Considering that only eighty-seven layers of the Tsukuyomi Academy Dungeon had been cleared at this point, their appraisal might have actually been reasonable... The four rings were strong items up until midgame. They did fall off near the end, though.

"With my low appraisal level, I can't really tell much about them," Sis prefaced, before giving us a simple rundown of her appraisal results. But I, of course, already knew everything about them.

Hatsumi explained that she felt fire energy from the red jewel, water energy from the blue jewel, wind energy from the green jewel, and earth energy from the yellow jewel. She couldn't get a good handle on the shabby ring, but compared to the other four, it contained only lower levels of mana.

I made sure she was done talking and took the four pieces of jewelry in my hand. Then I started passing them out to the four girls, matching them with the elemental they had the most affinity with.

To Nanami went the ring with the red, ruby-like jewel. She was well-rounded in all elements, but right now she was defaulting to fire a lot, so it made sense.

To Yukine went the ring with the deeply blue jewel, the color of sapphire. It was the optimal choice, given her affinity with the water element.

To Ludie went the emerald-green ring, reminiscent of a lush forest. The princess was practically synonymous with the wind element. I'd be relying on her wind magic many more times going forward.

Finally, to Sis went the ring with the citrine-yellow jewel. I had no idea if she could use earth elements, but... It would have to do for now, right?

"I'll take this one," I said, picking up the grungy leftover ring.

"What? You're really fine with that, Kousuke?"

"...Is it really all right for us to have these?"

Ludie and Yukine protested, surprised.

"Compared to the others, this one's got almost no power."

Sis was exactly right. The one I'd picked was dubious in regard to its rarity and abilities when compared to the four elemental rings. However, it possessed a power I couldn't use—Find Traps. That being said, its ability was pretty weak, so it became useless by midgame, as both thief-class characters and Nanami possessed skills that rendered it obsolete.

Still, this is what I'd wanted. No, I *needed* to have it.

Besides. Items only showcased their maximum strengths in the hands of people who could get the most out of them. With my inability to use an elemental magic, the other treasures would've been wasted on me.

With everyone's permission, I stashed the ring away, just before Sis held her hand out to me.

"I don't go into dungeons."

After forcing her ring into my hands, she started patting my head. Why exactly was I getting stroked, I wonder...?

"......Let's leave."

Nodding at Sis's suggestion, all of us walked into the spatial magic circle meant to transport us out of the dungeon.

After using the magic circle and warping back to the warrior maiden statues, I suddenly realized something as I was heading outside:

"Whoops, my shoes are untied. Everyone go ahead, I'll catch up."

There was no reason to make them stop and stand here in this stuffy, dark, and cramped cave. Yukine and the others agreed and continued outside.

Just as I finished tying my shoes and thought about hurrying after them...

I saw my shadow materialize in front of me.

Light was streaming out from behind me. I filled my stole with mana as I headed toward the warrior maiden statues.

In the center of the three sculptures was a glowing ball, floating in the air. Its glow was blinding, until it finally dimmed, then split into three triangles.

Each floated over to one of the pedestals placed in front of the statues, where they then descended to the tops of them and faded entirely.

One of these shapes was pure white.

This triangle for concealing the most private of places had a faintly reflective sheen, perhaps from synthetic polyester fabric, with lace adorning the area. Its backside could safely be described as little more than string, so it was awfully questionable if it actually could conceal anything at all.

This was the risqué pair of panties belonging to Ludie, which I'd seared into my memory.

One of the other shapes was blue.

The cloth at the base was made of cotton, and the whole thing was of firm and solid build. Not suggestive in the slightest, these would properly obscure one's important parts.

The upper part of the base fabric was decorated with lace shaped like snowflakes, and the waistband featured white frills.

This was the refined pair of panties belonging to Yukine, which I'd seared into my memory.

The other triangle shape was black and pink.

It was something I had already held and felt with my own two hands.

This was the sexy pair of panties belonging to Sis; I could clearly recall everything about them, right down to their faint leftover warmth.

"Hoooo."

Calm down, Kousuke. I needed to get the present situation in order.

On each of the three pedestals was one of three pairs of women's underwear.

I gulped.

The violent pounding in my chest was like a car engine with the accelerator slammed to the floor. While repeatedly urging myself to stay calm, I timidly turned back toward the entrance of the cave.

Nobody was there.

"Did something happen?" asked Ludie, staring right at me.

I'd just started to head home after catching back up with everyone.

"Wh-what? No, nothing at all, obviously," I replied, feigning composure.

"Really? You just seem to have a different air about you than usual, I guess…"

Uh-oh, deep breaths. I needed to take deep breaths and calm myself.

"I'm just a little tired, that's all. I'll get my energy back in no time."

At my reply, Ludie didn't press me any further, despite the somewhat curious look in her eyes. However:

"Now then, what exactly were you going to use to get that energy, and where was it going to go, I wonder?"

My body reacted with a jolt. When I casually glanced beside me, I found Nanami waiting.

"There's no need to worry, Master."

I could tell just from looking at her.

I wanted someone, anyone, to tell me I was wrong.

But my heart was telling me it was true.

Nanami had noticed. She'd absolutely found me out.

"It'll be our little secret."

Chapter 4 (**Preparation**   Magical★Explorer)

Now that Ludie and the others had gotten ahold of their pre-order bonus rings, I was officially the weakest out of everyone connected to the Hanamura house. Actually, it was best to be clear about it. Ludie possessed power so far beyond any of the other first-years, it was ridiculous to even compare us. Maybe she had a higher chance of defeating Iori than I did? She was so strong that I gave the idea some serious consideration.

That being said, I couldn't stay behind her forever.

What I needed to do was prepare to power myself up. I'd gotten items ready for this. I also had Nanami to assist me.

With that out of the way, my top priority was skipping school to visit dungeons.

"Are you sure this is the right idea when tests are coming up?" asked Ludie, worried for me. But I honestly couldn't care less about them... Okay, if I was being *truly* honest, they were on my mind. It wouldn't hurt for me to do well on them. I wouldn't fail... Probably. At the very least, my grades would be better than Orange's or Katarina's. Maybe.

"Or so you say, but you actually mean a date with your maid, Nanami, then."

"I meant what I said..."

Now that I was ready to go, I invited Nanami to accompany me. She responded with a sigh.

"Allow me to guess what's on your mind, Master. Yesterday, you cleared a dungeon. Getting ahold of my striped panties made you intensely aroused..."

"*Bzzzzt!* Nooooope!"

I didn't think it was necessary to point out what she had gotten wrong.

"I'm gonna devote today to a one-man workout, heh-heh," she said, mockingly.

"You're not going to listen to what I have to say, are you?"

Also, when I thought over her last remark, I wanted to spend the next hour grilling her about what sort of "workout" she was talking about.

"I was simply joking, of course. You are really thinking of watching some videos while throwing back a cold one and eating some sushi, right?"

"Am I a dad now? Some middle-aged dude, worn out from work?"

"Then perhaps you're going to use your annual pass to Tsukuyomi Fun Park and stuff your face while getting your fill of all the rides?"

"Now what am I supposed to be, a single woman in her thirties? Getting excited for a long weekend?"

"Then we'll meet in the middle and say it's a date with me."

"Yeah, right. 'In the middle.' More like flying off in a whole nother direction."

"You only need to bring you and your body along. For clothes... Well, we'll be walking around outside, so they won't really be necessary."

"Arrest me, officer, I'm right here!"

When I questioned what exactly her goal was here, Nanami heaved an exasperated sigh.

"It's very simple. What if, for example, you witnessed Miss Ludie clear a dungeon the day before, only for her to spar with Miss Claris back at the house and spend all night absorbed in her research?"

"You're just describing what I did yesterday..."

"Miss Ludie looks a bit tired and worn out, and yet despite it all, she's trying to head back into a dungeon. You'd stop her, of course, wouldn't you, Master? That's what I'm doing now."

Ah, I got it. Yeah, I'd definitely stop her if I was in that position. Even if it wasn't me, Sis or Marino or even Yukine or Nanami would stop her, too.

"So what you're saying is everyone's worried about me, is that it?"

"That is correct. You understand what I am getting at, yes?"

Yeah, yeah, I got it. That explained why she'd brought up going on a date with her out of the blue. She was trying to say that I should take the day off from dungeon-crawling and spend at least a day relaxing, whatever shape that took.

Nanami smiled an angelic smile. Oh right, she *was* an angel!

"Now then, let's get you out of those clothes."

"That's a bit of an odd conclusion to come to, wouldn't you say?"

I took back my statement about her being angelic. Why exactly did she have a huge grin plastered across her face? Whatever the case, the fact remained that my behavior was worrying her. Oh well, some downtime couldn't hurt.

"I guess I could take a day off. I am a bit tired, that's for sure."

At my reply, Nanami's eyes widened.

"What's wrong?"

"Oh, you simply acquiesced faster than I had expected. In the worst-case scenario, I was worried you would go off to challenge the dungeon solo instead."

Considering how I had acted up until now, that was a distinct possibility. I was beginning to wonder whether I spent more hours in hostile mazes than I did at home.

"While I'm grateful for everyone worried about me, I don't really think there's anything to complain about in what I'm doing."

Moreover, the thing I needed to do in the next dungeon was called an exploit. Activating it on my own was very inefficient, so I'd been planning to ask someone I knew to come with me.

Nanami was probably the only person I knew who would eagerly slip out of class to come along, though.

"I'll relax today, but I'm counting on you tomorrow, Nanami."

"Of course, as long as you recharge your artilleries and rest easy."

"That's technically one definition of the word, sure, but hearing you put it like that conjures up a vague sense of dread."

That aside, the issue of today's activities still remained.

"What exactly am I supposed to do then?"

I spread out my arms to play up being at a loss.

"In that case...," Nanami began. "Is there anywhere you would like to go, or something you want?"

"Somewhere I want to go, huh...?"

Well, I did have a few things I wanted. Namely, some items I needed to get ready before I took on the Tsukuyomi Academy Dungeon. I could take the opportunity to wrap that up now. That meant going to...

"The city. Gonna hit up a shop that deals in magic stones. You in?"

"But of course," Nanami replied, before clapping her hands together and gasping with realization.

"What, then, will you wear for your outfit? It's warm today, and the skies are clear, so perhaps nu—"

"I ain't going out the door in the buff, okay?!"

After getting ready to go out, I looked around our meetup spot and found that Nanami was already there. When she spotted me coming over, she ran off and hid in the bushes for some reason.

I had a bad feeling about this. It might've been best to turn right around and go off shopping on my own. Still, this was, technically, where we were meeting up.

"My humblest, *hngaah*, *haah*, apologies, *hnah*, *hnah*, for keeping you waiting, Master, *hnah*, *hnah*. ♪"

"Who're you supposed to be...? Your whole personality's different. Heck, you got here before me anyway, right?"

She'd been absentmindedly fiddling with her Tsukuyomi Traveler but ran off to hide the moment she saw me.

"What ever could you be referring to, Master? Of course I did not get here before you."

She nonchalantly adjusted her expression; the aloof Nanami I knew had returned.

"Well, Master. I have gotten myself properly dressed up for our day together. What do you think, does it suit me?" Nanami asked.

"......"

I gave her a once-over. She looked the same as always and was wearing her usual maid uniform. I got the feeling nothing about her was different from normal, or even different from when we talked earlier that day. Just what part of her was "properly dressed up"?

She was definitely fishing for a witty comeback to her setup. In any case, it was annoying that she put the onus on me to come up with something here, so I elected to give a vague answer to smooth things over.

"You look great."

"Right? Right? They were fairly expensive, but I am glad I bought them."

She was talking about her clothes, right?

"Ahh, no wonder they look so beautiful."

"Yes, I am quite fond of them myself. They raise one's defense as well, so putting them over the head might be a good idea, too."

"That does seem beneficial."

"Indeed, indeed. I do apologize for being so bold, but would you like to try them yourself, Master?"

"Yeah, definitely, if the need arises."

"Oh no, hearing you say that is a bit embarrassing. Not only complimenting my panties so highly, but even saying you'll wear them on your head, well..."

"We were talking about panties?!"

I was just randomly going along with the conversation, and now I'd gotten turned into a panties-loving pervert! Like hell there'd ever be a chance for me to wear them on my head!

"I did not think you would compliment them so much, when you cannot even see them."

That was because I didn't even consider that she was talking about her panties. Oh well, my best bet was to just go along with the gag.

"It's true, but I guess somewhere along the way I managed to gain X-ray vision."

Was I some eroge protagonist? This was an eroge world, so it wouldn't be strange to have X-ray vision, honestly. Though, wait a minute, what were we doing here, exactly?

"Enough of the jokes, let's get going."

"Yes, let us be off."

We both began walking. As we left the vast Hanamura property and approached the residential area, Nanami spoke up:

"By the way, Master. I would like it if you and I shared the same values."

What exactly was she getting at? For the time being, when it came down to whether I wanted to share that with her or not...

"I guess I think the same thing?"

Nanami nodded.

"I sincerely apologize for bringing up such a serious topic."

"Why're you apologizing for a *serious* topic...? Anyway, I don't think that's necessary."

Nanami suddenly held out her hand. There was something on her left ring finger. The ring I'd given her. Why had she chosen that specific finger to put it on?

"What are your thoughts on this ring, Master?"

The ring, then?

"…What sort of answer are you looking for, exactly?"

"What I want to know is its value. I do not understand just how much it is worth."

As I struggled to formulate an answer, she continued:

"I am aware that you do not wish to talk about yourself in detail, so I ask this bearing that in mind. If you do not wish to answer, I will not inquire any further," Nanami said, looking at the band on her finger. "That being said, I was left with a question after yesterday's events— why exactly was everyone so surprised at a ring with only this much power?"

The inlaid gemstone shone in the light.

"Miss Ludie, Miss Yukine, and even Miss Hatsumi, all sensed so much value in this ring's abilities."

When I thought back on it, Nanami was the only one among the group who hadn't been surprised by the treasure.

"Yet you were different, Master. You had the same reaction as I did."

She let out a sigh.

"If your reaction had been in line with everyone else's, such questions likely would not be on my mind. I could have understood that people simply value things differently."

But I had thought that the rings weren't worth much.

"Now, to my main point. Master, you did not intuit the same amount of value from the rings as everyone else, correct? Your estimation of their value aligned with mine instead of the other girls'."

"So basically, you're saying that I don't think those rings are as valuable as everyone else does?"

"Yes, that is exactly right. Why, then? If you cannot answer, then I'll have to…"

I couldn't help but smile.

"It's okay, it's okay. You got it right."

After all, this accessory was just something to tide the player over from the early game to the midgame.

"I don't sense much value from these things."

"…I had debated whether I should ask you directly or keep this question to myself."

She must have held back because it seemed like it would get down to the core subject I couldn't bring up with her yet.

"Look, if something's bugging you, you can always ask. I trust you.

As long as it's not something really out there, I'll give you an answer. Besides."

"Besides what?"

"I will definitely tell you everything at some point. I just need you to give me a bit more time."

At least until the Saraquel event was over. I didn't want to do anything until then.

"I bet you'll be surprised by tomorrow's dungeon. I mean, in a different way from this recent case with the rings, too. I hope you're excited."

Preparations to exploit the system.

"Then, I shall look forward to it."

With all of that settled, Nanami and I headed to the bonus dungeon included as a pre-order bonus from industry giant, ComfyMap.

This Ancestral River Pool was in the same level range as the panties dungeon, Gloomy Ruins, and the Twilight Cavern, where I'd met Nanami.

However, there were monsters here that were a full level higher than anything in those other dungeons.

But those higher-level monsters didn't show up like normal.

How did they show up, you ask? Why, by activating a trap, of course.

"Here I go, Master."

"Yup."

Nanami activated the trap, and a monster dropped down from the sky. It kicked up a cloud of dust and sent a heavy *thud* echoing around us as it connected with the ground.

This creature was called a gidiao. To put it simply, it basically resembles a giant turtle. About the size of a microcar, give or take. Despite its appearance, it's actually a type of dragon. On closer inspection, it has sharp claws on its hands and feet, and certain parts of it are covered with scales.

During my first playthrough, I'd rushed head-on at a gidiao without knowing how strong they were and got my whole party wiped out. It was only thanks to its slow walking speed that I somehow managed to make it out alive. I ran away as fast as I could, biting my lip and giving a final parting shout: "You haven't seen the last of me!"

Only later would I learn that there was a correct way to work through the dungeon.

That gidiao wasn't an appropriate level for this dungeon. It was a special monster that was several levels above the others and only came out of traps. If you visited the dungeon at the level it was suited for, it was impossible to beat. To stand a chance of taking it down, you'd normally have to raise your level.

But what were you supposed to do if you accidently stepped on the trap and made the gidiao show up? Given its slow speed, running away was the correct option.

However. While there was no arguing that running away was the proper move, was encountering a difficult enemy after stepping on a trap truly a dire situation?

Crisis generated opportunity. Depending on how efficiently you handled things, you could change bane to boon.

It was time for a change in perspective.

Traps, of course, are malicious things. But how beautiful would it be if you could take advantage of them? Currently, the device before us caused a monster, worth a good number of experience points, to appear in a low-level dungeon. One factor behind my growing appreciation for traps as an adult is how you can leverage them for your benefit. That isn't quite enough to offset my hatred of them, though.

Now, what did I need to do to make good use of this thing?

First of all, while we could definitely summon a monster from the trap, were we actually going to be able to take it down?

As it turned out, killing it was far from impossible, even at lower levels.

One of the big reasons *Magical ★ Explorer* became so popular was its game balance and well-designed weakness system. Though there were a few bosses without any deficiencies. Nevertheless, this turtle had a weakness. So long as you came up with a well-thought-out strategy to exploit it, even lower-level parties could beat it.

Right, it could be defeated. If I was able to mitigate the risks and take it down, it would be quite the wonderful way to farm experience points.

Nanami stared at the monster in shock. That was to be expected, really. Ostensibly, this was my first time coming to this dungeon, so why would I be aware that you could exploit its traps to level grind?

She was already close to figuring out the truth about me on her own, so I imagine this just made her even more suspicious. Despite that, she wasn't asking me about it. She was probably keeping quiet on purpose, believing I would explain everything to her eventually.

At any rate, Nanami wasn't the issue here. No, the issue was our target.

"This is gonna be a real pain…"

The next instant, I used my Third and Fourth Hands to flip the gidiaos on their backs as they descended from the ceiling. Once they were all lined up, legs flailing in the air, Nanami activated the trap again.

I flipped over the next batch of turtles as they fell to render them powerless, then lined them up in a row.

When we'd amassed a fair number of them together, Nanami used Explosive Arrow to blast their stomachs, while I set a punch into their gut to defeat them. I punched the next one in the gut and sent it packing.

In the game, I'd used this area as a farming spot. I'd cast earth magic to flip the gidiaos over and immobilize them, then attack them all at once or hit their stomachs for extra damage. This method worked here, too, which made things a breeze. There was just one little problem…

It was so dang boring.

Anyone would get sick of doing this over and over again. When I was at home alone, I'd watch videos while I did it, which wasn't so bad. When I speedran the game, I'd be streaming and reading the comments from viewers in the chat to make it more tolerable.

"Nanami, you know what I'm thinking right now?"

Keeping up her poker face, she continued to robotically fulfill her part of the workload.

"Naturally, I have a perfect understanding of your thought process, Master. You're thinking, *Man, I'd like about two more pairs of Nanami's used panties.* Correct?"

"Not even a little."

Why on earth would I be thinking something like that? Though, if you asked me whether I needed them or not, there was really only one answer.

"Yes, yes, one for safekeeping, one to admire, and one to wear yourself. It makes three the ideal number, does it not?"

"Not even a smidgeon."

Hearing her put it like that, though, three pairs did seem convenient...... Wait, where the hell was my mind going?

"One pair to put on yourself, one to wear over your head, and one to hold up high in the sky, then?"

"Not even one speck on the mark."

What were these, her version of the three sacred treasures? Truly off the pervy deep end. Boy, she really loved the "wearing panties on your head" bit, didn't she?

"No, you're not planning on using them to spread the faith, are you?!"

"Spread what faith?! And where?! Of course not!"

"Thank goodness, it would bring me nothing but pain to share them with anyone besides you, Master."

"Wait, so I'm okay then...?"

Hmm, well, it was hard to put into words, but I was a little happy to hear that.

Even during our nonsensical bantering, we kept our hands moving. Nevertheless, it didn't make the task any less of a slog.

Falling turtles.

Me, flipping them on their shells.

More falling turtles.

Me, flipping them on their shells.

Once a bunch were piled up, an Explosive Arrow and a gut punch.

Were we just gonna keep going and going...?

"We're gaining magic particles at a steady clip, here. Let's keep this up."

I nodded at Nanami's statement.

"Yeah, you're right......"

It was obnoxious, but when I thought about the future, this work was necessary. I needed to bulk up with all these particles.

We continued grinding for several hours, taking a few breaks along the way, until we finally decided to put an end to our turtle hunt.

The farming was excellent. I could acutely sense the stat raises I'd gotten from gathering all that experience. As I punched the turtles in the stomach, I'd gradually needed to put less and less force into them. Now I thought I could manage farming them solo, without the help of Nanami's Explosive Arrow. Still, two people were better than one here, because you could complete the task of tipping them over and lining them up much more efficiently.

"What should we do now?" Nanami asked, but there was only one real answer.

Deep in the dungeon was a boss eagerly awaiting our arrival. Behind it sat a treasure chest, too. However, while the item inside it would be great for Iori, it wouldn't be much use to me. Plus, the boss had a ton of HP, but was actually weaker than gidiaos we'd farmed. Bearing all this in mind, I arrived at my conclusion.

"Okay, let's leave the boss alone and head home!"

Nanami was dumbfounded, but I wasn't interested in fighting the boss at all. And why would I be? There was no reason for me to go down there.

If there had been a special bonus for clearing the dungeon, I might have gone to fight it. But this wasn't going to stamp a "Completed" mark on my map or anything, and even if I went farther into the dungeon, there were almost no rewards in either experience or skills for me to obtain.

Could I really stand to waste my time like that? During speedruns of a certain game, a town is attacked and transformed into a sea of fire, but on top of completely ignoring the event to save time, runners have no qualms about stealing items and money from the villagers' houses to go sell at a different town down the line. Compared to something like that, this was an unbelievably civilized way of saving time.

Besides, my schedule was already set in stone. I would go home, do my usual practice swings, and take a shower. Playing games or laughing along to funny videos with Ludie and the others in my spare time afterward would both be a nice chance of pace, a hundred times more meaningful than fighting a worthless monster. I didn't feel the slightest bit obligated to claw my way to the boss.

"All right, ready to get going?"

At that, Nanami took a circular item out from the pocket of her maid uniform and filled it with mana to activate it.

—Ludie's Perspective—

Dinner was over. I was gathering my notes together to help Katarina with her studies when I received a message from Marino.

She told me she had something to talk to me about.

It was rare for Marino to call me. I quickly cleaned up my notebooks and headed for the living room.

There were already a few people there, one of whom wasn't a member of the Hanamura household at all.

"Yukine?"

She gave a big smile at my inquiry.

"Evening, Ludie."

"You were called here, too?"

She turned to me and nodded as I sat down next to her.

"Yup, I was. A message showed up out of nowhere from the principal."

Yukine glanced at Marino, who proceeded to finish her conversation with Nanami and looked our way.

"Looks like everyone's here! ♪"

I glanced around the room. Six people were gathered there: Marino, Hatsumi, Yukine, Nanami, Claris, and me. Considering his absence, I could deduce what the subject of our conversation would be.

This was about Kousuke.

"Now, I imagine there're some of you who've figured this out already, but this is about Kousuke."

I was right. Everyone here carried some degree of feelings for him. Myself included.

"In fact, I've determined that Kousuke intends to do something crazy, extremely dangerous, and absolutely absurd! ♪"

I caught myself frowning as I listened to Marino.

"Really...?"

"Yup. And Nanami dearest and I... Huh, what? You don't want me to call you that? Just your name? But that's so cold and unfamiliar... Oh, c'mon, don't glare at me like that."

Nanami would get mad at me when I was too formal with her, or didn't call her by a nickname, so why was she so intent on having Marino do the opposite?

"*Ahem*. After consulting with Nanami, I've decided to lend my aid to Kousuke's efforts."

I stared blankly at Marino before eventually coming back to my senses. That boy planned on making some sort of trouble. And big trouble at that.

"Principal, what exactly is he trying to do?"

Marino beamed in response to Yukine's question.

"Apparently, he's planning to get top marks in his class by skipping exams. He even wants to set a record in the process."

I cocked my head at Marino's explanation.

"Skip the exams and earn the top spot in the class? Is that even possible?"

Just as I asked that...

"......I get it."

"I understand, skip them entirely...... I never considered doing it that way."

Hatsumi and Yukine both replied knowingly. I couldn't really get a read on Hatsumi, but Yukine nodded along, seemingly convinced.

"He'll really pull it off, too, is the thing..."

Claris also seemed curious; she was putting her hands on the table and leaning forward slightly.

"How will he do that, exactly...?" I blurted out.

"Ah, you haven't taken exams, so you've never seen the rankings board. It'd be impossible to imagine how in that case. But take them once, and you'd realize."

"Riiight, if you take them once, it gets pretty clear. Ludie. You know what the conditions for graduating from our school are, right?"

"Yes. Earning credits from required courses or clearing down to the sixtieth layer of the Tsukuyomi Academy Dungeon... Wait, you don't mean...?"

The thought suddenly crossed my mind. Was she referring to the sixty-floor graduation track?

"Yes, what you're imagining is likely correct. Grades at Tsukuyomi Academy are determined by both test scores and the lowest level of the dungeon you've cleared."

Now things were starting to make sense. This meant that Kousuke could still get the top grade in the class while skipping his exams. He just had to challenge the dungeon instead.

"Principal. I have a question," Yukine began. "Dungeon achievements are weighted highly, so he should be able to easily take top of his class by clearing ten-odd floors. But then, why did you imply he was trying to do something dangerous and absurd?"

"I was wondering about that, too. Kousuke could easily do that right now."

Marino nodded along to Yukine's and Hatsumi's points.

"True, true. I suspected myself that he could get through the first twenty layers, the ones the first-years should look to clear by the end of the year, whenever he wanted. The thing is, Kousuke's got his sights set somewhere much deeper than that..."

Marino sighed a little. Nanami continued where the other woman had left off.

"Master was exceedingly flippant when he mentioned it. That he would clear forty layers solo."

Yukine jumped up from her seat with a clatter.

"You're kidding!! *Forty* layers?!"

"......Unbelievable."

Meanwhile, the normally expressionless Hatsumi had a tinge of shock on her face.

"Um, just how much of a feat is getting down to the fortieth layer, exactly?"

Claris asked my question for me. Yukine took a deep breath before slowly beginning her explanation.

"The fortieth layer is the goal for us second-years. There are several students, including myself, who have already gotten that far. But it's definitely not possible on someone's first dungeon visit, that's for sure. And solo on top of all that...?"

"Absurd and reckless. Is Kousuke stupid?"

"I had the same reaction. Laughed it off as totally impossible. He even guffawed along with me, you know…"

All of a sudden, Marino's smile disappeared.

"But that look he had in his eyes. He was serious."

"I would say Master is certain to try."

Marino nodded at Nanami's comment.

"Yes, I'd say you're right there. I even thought to myself, why, maybe it'd be best to have him fail big-time for once. But the thing is, it appears Kousuke doesn't plan on just getting smacked around down there, either."

"Presently, Master is visiting a dungeon, gaining power at an unusual rate. I've been lucky enough to get the leftovers from this process as well."

"Nanami is right; Kousuke is growing stronger by the day. That's why, well, I started to think…"

Marino didn't voice the rest of her thought. Still, I understood what she was trying to say.

"But there's still another problem with what he's trying to do here."

"……I know. The time frame."

Yukine gave a shout of realization at Hatsumi's comment.

"That's right! Since the test results get announced school-wide, he'd only have about a week to do it all…! The Tsukuyomi Academy Dungeon's entry ban is being lifted on the first day of exams this year. From there, the testing period lasts a total of five days, and the scores are posted three days after that. His plan is totally impossible. Does Takioto have any idea? Each floor is a heck of a lot bigger than the dungeons we've been through before!"

I had figured as much. Taking the top grade in the class by clearing forty layers would mean he would finish everything by the time the exams scores were tallied and reflected in the class standings.

"Yes, you're right. The fastest student record was set by Yukine, Shion, and Fran with the former presidents of the three committees backing them up. Even then, it took six months from their first visit. Everyone says that it's unlikely to ever be broken."

Claris shouted with surprise when Marino said that.

"I-it takes that long to get through, and he's trying to do it in a week?!"

"How does Takioto plan to pull it off…? When we cleared it, we had class and other commitments, so we'd challenge it every once in a while, call it quits, then jump back in again a few days later, taking six months to work through it little by little. That still managed to beat the previous record by three months. Simply adding up all the time we spent inside the dungeon itself, it'd probably come out to at least a few weeks. But accomplishing all that in a week? And solo?"

"Un...believable............"

It must have been quite a feat to leave Hatsumi and Yukine so flabbergasted.

"I suggested he bring someone else along, too. Honestly, I'd like him to go with Ludie, Yukine, Nanami, any of you dea—*ow*, don't kick me! Any of you three. But it appears that this time, he just has to do things solo for some reason. He wouldn't even tell me why, either."

"Master's train of thought is on a higher level... No, it would be safe to say it is on a different dimension, far beyond either Marino's or my own understanding. However, that is precisely why I believe..."

Nanami scanned over the room with a solemn look in her eyes.

"...that Master will be able to pull it off."

"Nanami and I have decided to cheer him on. I'm still technically a teacher, though, so I can't give him special treatment and can only cooperate to a certain extent...," Marino said before looking at Yukine and me.

"See, that's why I want everyone's help. I know you both have your exams coming up, but I'd still like you to be there for him. Please, I beg you."

Marino bowed. However, such a gesture was wholly unneeded.

"Please raise your head up. I'd be there for Kousuke, even if you didn't ask."

Hearing my reply, Yukine chuckled.

"Same goes for me, too."

At our replies, Marino raised her head and stood up abruptly. Then, a smile slipped onto her face.

"These are your first exams, too, Ludie. Forgive me. And you, too, Yukine."

Marino approached us and put her hands on Yukine's shoulders.

"Thank you for being there for him going forward. Oh, I've got it. If coming out this far is too much trouble, you could always live here if you'd like. I'm sure you'll end up here eventually, anyway."

Wait, "end up here eventually"? What was she talking about? Yukine and I turned to each other and cocked our heads in confusion.

"Oh, that reminds me, Yukine. One other thing."

"Yes? What is it?"

"I think Kousuke's already figured out what sort of roles you all have. That's why he's purposefully trying to stand out."

Marino's supposition left Yukine bewildered. But soon she grasped what the other woman meant and gave a strained smile.

"Really? It's a little bit disappointing to think about it like that."

"It's pretty much the case, I imagine... Still."

"Yes, the relationship between the two of us won't change. If anything, it means we'll only be more involved with each other going forward."

I hadn't the faintest idea what they were talking about. I was going to ask Yukine for clarification, but...

"Sorry, Ludie dear. I can't talk to you about it right now. But I'm sure you'll find out about it soon."

Marino cut me off before I could ask anything.

"That's true. In fact, I can guarantee it. You'll know about it for certain after exams are over. I'll be coming to talk to you about it myself."

I couldn't help getting even more curious, but her words left me with no choice.

"I understand. Then... I'll ask you about it when the time comes."

"Now, that should be everything. Yukine, go ahead and spend the night here. Would you mind helping her get settled, Claris?"

"Leave it to me."

We then all exited the room. I decided to leave Yukine with Claris and head to my room for the time being... Actually, was it all right to put everything on her?

A question was still lingering in my mind. After all, there had been times lately where Yukine seemed to have her mind on something else.

If you asked me which people most stood out on the Tsukuyomi campus in *Magical★Explorer*, I would have immediately nominated two people for the distinction. The reason was simple: They clearly had the strangest getups in the Academy.

One of them I had yet to meet, but I'd already laid eyes on the other. The vice-minister (vice presidential role) of the Ceremonial Committee, Shion Himemiya.

The strange thing about the Japanese-style clothing she wore was that it scarcely resembled a uniform. This flew in the face of the otherwise standardized Academy uniforms. Apparently, students weren't actually required to wear a uniform. It impressed me how she'd rejected the outfit almost every other student wore to stay true to herself.

It was easy to tell from Shion's beautiful and dignified demeanor that she had lived a life of privilege from a young age. Considering she was also tall for a girl, it made her stand out all the more. She was like a single, tall, pink chrysanthemum in a field of dandelions—conspicuous enough that you could single her out even from quite far away. Students would also actively move away from her out of their disdain for the Ceremonial Committee, which only amplified her striking presence.

However, if asked whether she stood out the most *right now*, that might not necessarily be the case.

Shion absolutely stuck out. Her idiosyncratic personality also helped her easily leave an impression. But now that I'd seen her in real life, I couldn't necessarily say she stood out the most.

What I felt much more keenly after living in the world of *Magical★ Explorer* was that Ludie stood out on campus far more than I ever would've imagined. On top of being a member of the Tréflc Empire's imperial family, she was unbelievably attractive. She'd been destined to end up the talk of the school, so the creation of the LLL fan club had been nothing but a matter of time.

That being said, the LLL fan club had agreed to support her from the shadows to ensure she could enjoy a healthy and tranquil daily life. Hence why they tried not to approach her needlessly. But when you combined that with her already highest of highborn status, it meant few people approached Ludie besides her close friends.

As such, the area around her person had transformed into a strange space, like some sort of holy ground. The same thing had happened for Student Council President Monica, so her presence was extremely conspicuous.

However, a few new faces had appeared recently that were gathering just as much, if not more, attention as these girls.

They were a two-person group. One was a boy. He was the subject of brutal gossip in certain sections of the student body. Anyway, this male student wore a stole that was stupid big, larger than the average person was tall, and could often be found chatting with Princess Ludie.

Nevertheless, he'd been skipping class a lot lately, so people were saying his presence was beginning to fade. I'd heard that when this guy finally showed up for the first time in a while, he had a drop-dead gorgeous silver-haired girl dressed up like a maid with him. And apparently, the uniform wasn't just for show—she was really devoted to attending and caring for this guy. Who the hell were these two, anyway?

That would be us.

"Hey, doesn't it feel like everyone's sorta distancing themselves from us and staring? And, uh, gossiping about you?"

Iori was spot on—all eyes in the cafeteria were on us. It was like we were in a zoo. With us in the enclosures, obviously.

I figured my stunningly beautiful maid, Nanami, was drawing more eyes than me, but she seemed to be ignoring it entirely. If anything, she was enjoying the situation.

To the point where she made a big display of devotedly looking after me.

Which was all well and good, but, you know, I wished she wouldn't loudly shout things like, "You want to rest your head on my lap?!"

Scratch that, she was *definitely* having fun with it. Though I did get a little pleasure out of watching flabbergasted students whip their heads around to look at us.

Maybe later on, back at the house, I could quietly lay my head on her lap and have her clean my ears or...... Nah, I could never ask her to do something so embarrassing.

Well, it only made sense that acting like this would draw attention. If the situations were reversed, I'd probably be staring and gossiping, too. Wishing I could trade places.

"...My bad, Iori. You can keep your distance from me; I won't mind."

As I spoke, a cup of coffee was placed down in front of me. Nanami had apparently been thoughtful enough to prepare some.

She set another cup in front of Iori and started placing star- and moon-shaped pieces of sugar beside it. 1, 2, 3, 4, 5, 6, 7, 8, 9, 10 pieces of sugar.

"Thank you," Iori smiled, before picking up the moons and stars. Just as I was about to laugh and call out Nanami for bringing too much sugar, Iori poured all ten pieces into his cup.

Aww, he wooks so happy dwinking his coffee-woffee.

"I can keep my distance…? What the heck are you talking about, Kousuke?"

Meanwhile, nothing but heart-shaped pieces of sugar had been heaped onto my plate, but I would've liked some stars and moons, too. None of that really mattered, but these sugar cubes were so cute, I would've loved to keep them for my own personal use. Couldn't we bring some back home?

"I know you're a really great guy, Kousuke, and besides, you're my friend. If you don't want to hang out with me, well…um, I'll go away, but…"

What was up with this dude?

"Iori, order whatever you want. As much as you want. From the top of the menu to the bottom, doesn't matter. I'll pay for it."

Sheesh, he was such a good dude…! He lent me his notebook whenever I'd skip class, too, but he should be working to score points on his tests, not score points with me. H-he could be as nice as he wanted; that still didn't mean I was going to let him have the title of strongest, you hear me?!

"F-friends don't do that! Besides, Kousuke, you're always sending me messages and introducing me to new dungeons!"

After chiding Iori to calm down, I ordered parfaits for him and Nanami. He declined my offer, but I insisted, convincing him I was paying him back for lending me his notebook. Naturally, the maid didn't hesitate to dig into hers.

No, Nanami, I wasn't look at you because I wanted you to feed me. Stop.

Though, if she was actually going to do that, I wouldn't refuse. Anybody'd be happy to have a beautiful maid scoop parfait into their mouth, right? Right?

I parted my lips, ready and waiting, and she silently picked up her spoon. But then, right as she brought it in front of my mouth, she arced it back and plopped it into hers.

She was good. I had to admit it.

"That reminds me actually, Kousuke, are you going be to okay during exams? You can count the days we have left on one hand, you know."

Iori gave a strained smile as I forcibly tried to snag a bite of Nanami's parfait.

"Nah, I'm not okay. But I'll be fine."

Because I wasn't going to take them in the first place.

For these past few days, after negotiating behind the scenes with Marino, I felt like I hadn't opened a single notebook or textbook at all. The only thing I had really been looking at was upturned turtle bellies.

I'd also asked her not to reveal this to Ludie and the others, so they wouldn't worry about me.

So why, pray tell, had she spilled everything to them all the very next day, then?

"Hmm? Katarina and the others are desperately studying in the library while Ludivine teaches what she can, you know? But... Well, thing is..."

I knew, he didn't need to say another word. That must've been why Ludie looked at her wit's end during breakfast this morning.

"It'll be fine. I'm gonna end up at the top anyway."

"Reeeeally?" Iori said, frowning.

"Of course, I'm serious, c'm—hmm? What, Nanami? Are you actually doing it for real this time?"

As I sat, mouth open, Nanami feeding me parfait, Iori, who'd been kindly watching along, suddenly gasped with realization. What the hell? Now I was embarrassed all of a sudden!

"Right, the library thing made me remember, but there's a librarian who's just as pretty as Nanami and Ludivine."

"Ahh, you mean Sakura?"

"Oh, so you're aware. Yeah, that's her. I don't know, I wasn't planning on borrowing any books, but she told me that I'd be using the library eventually, so I might as well register, and I signed up to use the place. She was so beautiful, I couldn't help staring at her."

"Really? Well, she is pretty, that's for sure."

Not that I had actually met her since coming to this world, though.

"So besides exams, how're things going? Like with dungeons and stuff."

"I'd say things are smooth on that front, too. Not with President Monica, herself, mind you, but I've been going through a bunch of dungeons with some of the people from the Student Council."

"Ohhh, not bad, not bad."

I was relieved. Iori seemed to be advancing through the Student Council route without any trouble. At this rate, he would be able to join the Student Council during the event that would come up a little bit after exams ended.

"It's all thanks to you, Kousuke. You've given me so much advice."

I suppose I had.

"Nah, I barely did anything, really. If things are going well for you, that's 'cause you worked so hard."

In actuality, I'd just picked out some dungeons from the ones he didn't know about that I thought he'd be best suited for and simply told him about them.

"Y-you think so?"

"I sure do."

"I'm happy to hear that. I've been really giving it everything I've got. And lately, things have been going well for me, too. It feels like I'm getting stronger."

So his talents were coming into bloom. I bet he'd be stupid strong by the time he joined the Student Council. Be that as it may, though...

"That's well and good, but I don't plan on falling behind."

"Well, I'm not planning on falling behind you, either."

Chapter 6 (**Yukine Mizumori of the Big Three** Magical★Explorer)

My upperclassman, Yukine Mizumori, was beautiful.

It wasn't only limited to her looks, either. Sure, she was physically attractive, but everything else about her was also gorgeous—the way she carried herself, the way she wielded her naginata, her way of seeing the world, and her soul.

"Did something happen, Yukine?"

Lately, however, she seemed to have somewhat of a cloud hanging over her.

Yukine smiled uncomfortably, scratching her head.

"What makes you say that?'

She was always zoning out. The swings of her naginata lacked their usual punch.

"Hmmm, well. I just thought your naginata work wasn't as elegant as usual."

I could tell after observing her for so long. She wasn't her usual self.

"Not as elegant, huh…?" Yukine replied, before lapsing into thought.

"Is there something troubling you?"

Yukine was debating whether to talk about it or not. She looked over at me, let out an uncertain groan, and grimaced. But then she finally pointed toward a rock that served as a perfect seat.

"I…have a bit on my mind right now."

We both sat down on the rock. Yukine's gaze was directed out at the waterfall.

"Something on your mind?"

I got the sense she was conflicted about something. Before long, she gave a sigh of resignation and smiled slightly.

"It's strange, really. Normally, I'd think this isn't something to talk to you about, but part of me also wants to tell you for some reason. I also have this bizarre feeling that I'd find the answer I'm looking for if I did."

I remained silent, and Yukine began speaking again. "Just how strong can I actually get? How far can I go?" She continued. "There's someone I've always seen as my goal, who I've never been able to best. Well, it's my own older sister, but… Once, she told me, 'Yukine, you'll be able to become the strongest in the world. So you should aim for that goal in my stead.' And I ended up promising her to do just that."

"…I think you could definitely be in the running for the most powerful in the world. Though, I'm going to get in the way of that."

"*Ha-ha*, let me finish… See, even as I grow older and mature, my big sister's always ahead of me. Despite the fact that she's not here anymore."

Yukine's big sister was dead. She'd expired in a horrible way, too.

"The thing is, after coming to the Academy and keeping up my own training, I laid eyes on President Monica and the principal. Learned people like that existed."

Her tone dropped.

"I can sort of understand that everyone's got expectations for me. Especially since some, like you, tell me that straight to my face. But I question if I'll be able to measure up to everyone's hopes for me."

I understood what was eating at Yukine. She lacked confidence. Her sister was holding her back. If I could free her of those worries…

"Though I was skeptical, I tried to grow stronger, even as my sister's words echoed in the back of my mind. But…"

"Yukine. Can I say something?"

I understood it all, even without her having to say it. I also knew what I needed to do. Now was the time to act.

"This might just be my own selfishness speaking. That's why there's something I'd like you to tell me."

I broke off and stared hard into Yukine's eyes.

"Do you want to get more powerful?"

Personally, I wanted her to be the absolute mightiest of all. Yukine Mizumori of the Big Three, who I loved so much. Yukine Mizumori, who I'd only grown to love more and more. But her own wishes took priority. It would be arrogant to push something she didn't want onto her. That was why I would ask first.

"Will I be able to?"

"You will. Powerful enough to eclipse whatever you think being the 'strongest' means. I know that the time leading up to exams is valuable, but... If you wouldn't mind... No, actually, I'd like you to come with me right now."

Yukine had exams coming up, and I had my dungeon challenge. But this was *her* we were talking about. She'd probably done most of her exam prep already. Unlike me, she was an honors student.

But this moment was as critical for me as it was for Yukine. An opportunity that would determine a number of important things from here on out, where I could show the results of everything I had worked for until now, knowing full well I'd be treated like an underachiever despite it all.

And above all else, this would help me grow. The timing was probably not perfect, but it wouldn't be an outright mistake to go now. More than anything, I wanted to prioritize helping my friend.

"Yukine... Let's visit a dungeon together."

—Yukine's Perspective—

It would be silly to ask how he knew of a dungeon that wasn't marked on the map. I already knew the answer: *Because it's Takioto.* I had faith in him, so that thought was enough to settle the matter.

If there was one thing I could say about him, it was that I could believe in him. Would he really do something that went against my own interests?

To that, I could give a resounding "no." Everything that had happened until now had proved as much. Though that didn't preclude him from putting me through the occasional embarrassing experience.

Dayspring Labyrinth.

That was apparently the name of the dungeon Takioto had brought me to. If you asked me what it looked like, I would likely have described it as a ruins-style dungeon carved from stone.

Takioto would occasionally introduce me to unique floors and dungeons, and this time was much the same.

"For a place called a labyrinth, it's not very much of a maze."

Nor were there any signs of monsters here, either.

"Not at all. This place is undoubtedly a labyrinth, in a certain sense. Because you have to conquer your own labyrinth to clear it."

"...Your own labyrinth?"

"That's right. Depending on the type of person you are, it can either be excruciating or a breeze. Putting it another way, you'll be able to fight against the strongest."

I puzzled over his vague statement, knowing he wasn't going to say anything more concrete.

"It's funny, isn't it? You can enter with a party, but each member goes off to fight on their own, anyway."

In other words, while you could challenge it with other people, your party would be split up along the way, and each individual would have to fight against a different monster by themself. According to Takioto, if you defeated your foe, it was possible to go over to your party members who had yet to get through their fight and lend them your aid.

Takioto also seemed to have an inkling of who he'd be going up against. He told me that he didn't know who I would fight. Still, judging by the way he spoke, I figured he definitely had some idea.

But that didn't mean he told me who it would be.

We advanced down an enchanted pathway and came upon a magic circle. Two of them, actually. In front of them was a message written in ancient script.

"It appears we'll each have to go on our own from here," Takioto smoothly commented, glancing at the circles. "That reminds me, Yukine. There's something I'd like you to remember."

"What's that?"

"You're absolutely capable of beating the enemy that will appear before you. I'm certain I'll defeat my own boss fast and will head over to where you are, but I'm not going lend a hand. Because you can absolutely win on your own."

"I can defeat it, no matter what?"

"That's right. Even if you start to lose faith in yourself. But you're not alone in that. This trial can make anyone nervous."

With this, Takioto took my hand.

"But you can overcome that. You absolutely can. Believe me. If it's impossible, and something happens to you, I'll look after you for the rest of my life. So I don't mind at all if you lose on purpose, either. Please face it with everything you've got."

Takioto stared at me hard in the face before suddenly letting go of my hand. He gave a simple, "I'm off," and stepped onto the left magic circle. I watched as he disappeared, then stepped onto the device in front of me.

A familiar locale greeted me on the other side. The waterfall I had begun using shortly after I entered the Academy.

The flowing stream, the chirping of birds, and the sound of water crashing down. The gentle wind that brushed my skin was slightly humid.

Unsure about what I needed to do, I decided to head behind the waterfall for the time being. As I made my way over, I saw it.

In the middle of the waterfall, atop a boulder large enough to fit several people at once, something was lingering.

A black shadow. But when I glanced at it again, it was the spitting image of the figure who'd been on my mind, day in and day out.

Indeed, it looked exactly like me with my hair down.

There was one clear difference. In her hand she held not a naginata, but a katana.

The shadow silently drew her sword and held it against me. That's when I realized.

I couldn't breathe right. I couldn't understand it.

Just why, how, what was happening? What was going on? This couldn't be happening; I couldn't believe it—

I continued to stare at the figure, and the emotions dwelling deep in my heart came spilling forth. I grew nauseous as the overflowing sensations mixed chaotically in my chest.

This shade wasn't me. It wasn't me at all.

I had seen her stance before. I had seen it countless times before, been compared against it countless times before, been tormented by it countless times before. She was the reason why I'd given up on the katana entirely.

"Suzune...... Is that you, Sis?"

The Dayspring Labyrinth was a dungeon you could challenge like normal; you didn't need to satisfy difficult conditions or download a special patch to unlock it. And though it triggered important events for certain characters, it was still a fundamentally optional dungeon.

Nor was it required to make the protagonist, Iori Hijiri, the strongest character.

But for Yukine Mizumori fans, it was a place they needed to visit at all costs. As long as Yukine herself didn't tell me it was unnecessary, I had always planned on coming here without any second thoughts.

Now, unlike normal dungeons, only one monster appeared per party member here. The labyrinth would pit your party members against the person they felt was strongest, or the person who had afflicted them with some lingering trauma.

For Yukine, that was her older sister. I couldn't think of anyone else it could be. That was a foregone conclusion.

Meanwhile, on my end, it was him, of course. I couldn't imagine facing off against anyone else.

I passed through the magic circle and found myself on the street I took to school every day.

The long-out-of-season cherry blossoms were blooming enough to pack the whole street, and their petals were falling down to the ground, at a rate of five centimeters per second.

After heading straight down the cherry blossom–lined road, I reached a familiar gate. Just like back then, it was closed tight. Standing before it was a shadow in the shape of a boy.

The shade wore a perfectly fitted school uniform. A dull hairstyle with a charming, androgynous face. The sort of unremarkable face you'd often find on eroge protagonists or no-name background characters.

"Figured it'd be you, Iori."

Iori Hijiri was barring my path.

The shadow Iori Hijiri didn't reply. He just stood stock-still, staring straight at me.

He wasn't smiling, like when he'd been eating a parfait. Nor was he wearing the look of concern he'd shown about the nasty things people were saying behind my back. He simply placed his left hand on his sheathed sword and looked ahead emotionlessly.

I filled my stole with mana and began to approach.

The Iori-shaped shade silently drew its sword and cast aside the sheath. Gravity then brought it down to the ground. Yet it made no sound. The instant it made contact with the street, it broke into small black particles and disappeared.

The shade pointed the tip of his blade straight at me.

I kicked off the ground and opened up my stole. Iori covered his right hand with a magic circle before pointing at me and firing.

"*Ha-ha.* Right, you can use magic, too."

Well, I suppose I had expected as much. I was up against the protagonist, a concentrated mass of possibility.

His fireball came flying straight at me. I knocked it aside with my Third Hand and took a step forward.

It wasn't just fire. Water, wind, earth, and even light. Judging by what I saw...

"So this is a Battlemage Iori Hijiri, huh?"

The protagonist contained infinite possibilities. He could specialize in physical attacks as a simple melee fighter just as easily as he could concentrate on magic attacks as a ranged caster. Although he couldn't match the Acting or Founding Saint, he could also use healing magic, on top of being able to use a variety of different weapons, from bows to spears to whips and more.

Of all the paths he could take, I believed the Battlemage build was his most balanced. He could flawlessly wield both magical and physical attacks, so it was quite flexible. The only drawback with the build was that it was easy to end up with a character who didn't excel at anything on your first playthrough. The fact that he'd still turn out above average at everything despite that was a testament to his power.

He definitely packed a punch, I had to admit.

"But this ain't Iori Hijiri."

There was no way; he'd never be so weak.

Nanami was about the only other character who could rival the number of different spells and skills at Iori's disposal. But I had a power that he didn't: the ability to manipulate my stole.

The real protagonist......was even mightier than this. He'd get stronger and eventually appear before me.

Could I really afford to lose to this thing? Could I really challenge greater heights if I faltered here?

Of course not.

"I've gotta crush him. Make it an overwhelming victory."

This was a shadow of Iori. Not the man himself. The Iori I had my sights on was the version of him who was strongest in the world.

Right now, the protagonist was slowly but surely growing in power. He was establishing a solid foundation.

Going forward, I planned on introducing Iori to more and more dungeons that suited him.

There was no question that I was strong right now. Indeed, I had been that way for a while. From here on out, though, Iori would begin to make a comeback for the ages. Heck, it would be trouble for me if he didn't. It was what I needed to lead all the heroines to their happy endings.

I needed to become even stronger, too.

That was why I was shooting to clear forty layers of the Tsukuyomi Academy Dungeon in a week.

"What? You're still here, doppelganger?"

The shade's magic was feeble. Its sword was weak.

I've already seen everything your blade has to offer. Something like you can't be Iori. How dare you try to imitate him.

Beneath the protection of my stole, I drew my sword and steadily drove the shade back.

I lost track of how many times we clashed. When the shade swung its blade down toward me, I parried with my stole and drew my weapon from its sheath as I rotated with the momentum.

The mana I'd built up exploded, cleaving the shade in two.

I didn't give it a second glance. I began walking toward the newly formed spatial magic circle.

To pull off the stupidly big goal I'd set for myself, I needed to get my hands on a particular item, and fast.

I wanted it above all else.

That was my reason for challenging the Tsukuyomi Academy Dungeon.

It would just take a single week. A long and excruciating one.

But that wasn't important right now. There was something else I needed to do.

"Time to join Yukine."

—Yukine's Perspective—

By the time I was aware of the world around me, I'd already internalized that I could never beat Suzune.

It was when I swung around a small stick, imitating my parents, who ran a dojo teaching swordplay and archery. I saw my two-years-older sister sparring with my father, which had spurred my desire to try fighting.

No matter how many times I tried, I never could beat her. My sister's amazing ability impressed me even as a small child. At the time, I thought that stemmed from the age gap between us.

However, I didn't need much longer to learn it was all my sister's talent and to decide that I would never surpass her for the rest of my life. As if to prove this truth, I would never once best my sister from that point onward.

The shade readied her katana, kicked the ground, and drew close in an instant. I gasped as I stopped the incoming blade with my naginata.

This *was* Suzune's swordplay.

The shade's weapon, the looming blade, bore a close resemblance to what lingering memories I had of her. The only difference was that this blade was even faster and even sharper.

Tempestuous, storm-tossed waves.

Suzune's chain of attacks fit that description perfectly. Holding out against the blade blitzing toward me took everything I had. When I tried to escape from the reach of her katana, the shade would immediately close the distance, as if to deny me even a moment's breath.

I blocked the attack with my scabbard, pushing back with force to knock the shade off balance.

Then, with my naginata still at the ready, I summoned a floating sphere of water and prepped an incantation.

At this, the shade put up its guard and watched, backing off from her advance and opening up space.

"It almost feels like I'm taking on President Monica."

At this rate, firing the Water Ball at her would be meaningless. Fully cognizant of this, I still tried sending it her way.

The shade didn't even try to dodge. She fixed her eyes on it and swung her katana. That was enough to rupture the Water Ball, splitting it in two.

Then, readying her sword once again as if nothing had happened, she slowly began to close in.

She had slowed down partway through. But that didn't last for long. The shade abruptly sped up and slashed at me.

By quickly picking up speed after lulling me with her gentle movements, she was trying to make it more difficult for me to react.

I blocked the blow. But it was a feint. The shadow kicked me in the stomach and sent me flying. Then, without a moment's delay, a magic circle materialized in front of her, and ice spears flew out of it toward me.

I immediately swung my naginata and knocked the spears out of the air.

Dodging the shadow's slash as she drew close, I then aimed at her forearm to take advantage of her momentary opening.

I felt it connect. Even I could tell I'd cut into it. However…

"Why…is she unharmed…?"

…the shade I thought I'd sliced into was completely unharmed.

Calm down.

I would slash her again. Simple as that. My opponent's movements were close to the movements of the Suzune I knew. So I would parry, dodge, and look for an opening.

"Not again."

I was sure the attack had landed. But I hadn't been able to slice my sister's doppelganger.

From there, even after slashing the shadow countless times, the results remained the same. It was like I was taking on a ghost that no blade could fell.

I couldn't come up with a way to deal with her. No matter how many times I thought I'd struck her down, the shade never yielded.

The shade was probably picking up on my unrest. I thought I saw her say, "The time has come." She then stepped toward me and peppered me with sword slashes. Her katana grazed my clothes at the same instant a rock she'd kicked struck my face.

Before I knew it, I was at a disadvantage. It was taking everything I had just to defend myself against her ceaseless, overwhelming blows.

In the end, this was how it always had been. No matter how much I strived, Suzune was always out there in front of me, along with President Monica. And Principal Marino far outstripped them both.

There was Shion and Fran beside me. Ludie and Takioto were coming up from behind. Every one of them possessed some irreplaceable gift or talent.

Why had my sister said I could become the best out there? I couldn't understand.

Ugh, had my naginata always been so heavy?

Did this shadow always loom so large?

The shade looked at me and lowered its sword for some reason. Had it finally decided I wasn't a worthy opponent? True, right now, I wasn't worth anything at all…

"Yukine!"

I wasn't sure when he'd shown up, but Takioto was now standing in the waterfall area where I had been teleported. He shouted at me. And then said no more. Nor did he show any signs of moving from that spot.

Instead, he just looked at me liked he wanted to say something. I already knew what that was. He didn't need to utter a word. Takioto believed in me.

Where exactly was his faith in me coming from?

I stared at his face and remembered what he'd said to me.

"Believe me. If it's impossible, and something happens to you, I'll look after you for the rest of my life. So I don't mind at all if you lose on purpose, either. Please face it with everything you've got."

"Ha-ha-ha."

Even with my sister standing in front of me, I couldn't help but laugh. The next thing I said slipped automatically from my mouth:

"You dummy. That line sounds straight out of a sappy romance novel."

Why then, I wondered.

Why did I feel so much power surging up within me?

I stared hard at the shade. This shadow was my sister. The sibling I couldn't overcome. However, the simple truth was that I had never overcome her *before*.

I was being watched. By Takioto, who'd tossed his reputation aside to keep challenging himself, who was here with me now.

Moments ago, I had been at a disadvantage. Yet for some reason, the feeling that I would lose never came. Instead, I felt that I couldn't let myself give in to despair at a moment like this.

Takioto had said that this battle could be difficult or a breeze, depending on the individual. That had to be a hint on how to approach the fight.

A thought came to me. Maybe my will, my desire to win this battle, was influencing the outcome. Since I had an inferiority complex toward my sister, I couldn't defeat her shade.

I had never once heard about a monster like this. Perhaps it didn't really exist, and it was just some nebulous presence that dwelled here. Dungeons were incomprehensible mysteries. Anything could happen inside their walls.

So what did I need to do? I had to believe I could win. But could I really beat my sister?

Suddenly, I remembered something Suzune had told me.

"Yukine. Everyone says I'm a genius, but the thing is, I'm just a person. And Yukine, you're..."

Right. She was right. My sister was a genius, but she was also human. And...

"I'm a person, too."

I was the same as her... There was no reason I couldn't surpass her.

I was going to show her everything I had.

If that still wasn't enough, I'd simply have Takioto take me in. Though, honestly, that sounded like it could be fun in its own right.

"Listen, Suzune. I've continued with my training even after your death. I've honed my skills."

I would show them off to her. I'd show them off to Takioto. This was the path I'd been going down. This was my technique.

Take a good look. This is who I am now. Yukine Mizumori.

Though she'd appeared to be losing ground, Yukine switched to the offensive after looking my way. The change was dramatic. Now the battle looked almost one-sided.

Maybe to some people, they might have seemed evenly matched.

Of the two, Suzune Mizumori was the one taking the offensive the most. But Yukine was evading all of her sister's blows with ease.

At this point, she had read all of her sister's attacks. No matter how many times the shade struck, she was never going to hit Yukine. I could tell.

"Hyah!"

This time, Yukine swung her naginata. Her attack had definitely caught the shade. However, the shadow quickly reformed her body and swung her weapon back.

In contrast to my surprise, Yukine looked on and laughed, as though celebrating her worthy opponent.

A feint weaved in with a flash of steel.

The shade was cleaved in two again before it brought its body back together once more. Even when Yukine struck it with magic, the doppelganger didn't seem the least bit damaged.

Despite it all, Yukine was smiling. Though her opponent appeared invincible, she didn't show the slightest hint of backing down.

Yukine flourished her naginata.

These slashes were somehow different from the ones that had come before. Something had changed, as if she was putting her whole essence behind each individual attack. The power behind them had changed, too.

I couldn't get her moves out of my head. They didn't look like regular old attacks to my eyes.

It was no exaggeration to say they were works of art.

Cutting downward, slicing upward, thrusting. Sidestepping, parrying, blocking.

Some might watch her movements and think she was dancing. However, I didn't think she was dancing at all.

Yukine was painting a picture, using her body and naginata as the brush.

Each individual movement was beautiful. If I could preserve these instances, like you do when you photograph something, each would be as stunning as the work of a master painter.

Right when Yukine repelled Suzune Mizumori's weapon with an upward slash, I suddenly remembered something she'd told me once.

"This is true of swords, katanas, and naginatas as well, but there's a heart that dwells within the flash of a blade."

Yeah, that had to be it. There was a heart dwelling in the blade glinting before my eyes.

Yukine's beautiful heart, her foolishly straightforward spirit, was etched in the flashes of her blade.

Simple yet harsh, but filled with an almost transparent beauty, they left behind an echoing afterimage each time she finished her stroke.

The glinting of her naginata, violent and mighty, yet filled with beauty, was almost like…

"A dragon. Inside those slashes…dwells a dragon."

It was fair to say I was totally captivated.

I wanted to swing my own sword as beautifully as Yukine did. But could I replicate her skills in my own katana technique?

At this point, it was impossible to even imagine she could lose this battle.

Then, in the middle of combat, Yukine took her eyes off her opponent and glanced toward me. It was a single second. Still, I understood what she wanted to say.

"*Take a good look.*"

Yukine stared down the shade in front of her, a solemn look on her face, and cloaked her whole body in mana. The shade drew in close, and right as it swung its sword down, Yukine launched her attack.

The scene took my breath away.

My heart was pounding. A warm substance welled up in the corner of my eyes. How could I not cry when I was gazing at such a brilliant work of art?

She loosed a repeated series of dazzling, lightning-fast slashes. But, in each one, I could see a dragon. The dragon that dwelled within them.

Well, Yukine had gone and learned it already. As of this moment, she'd mastered that technique.

The technique. Synonymous with the Water Dragon Princess of the Big Three, whom I adored.

Yukine Mizumori, master of martial art.

And the attack that eventually leads to the ultimate secret skill that cements her as a pillar of *Magical★Explorer*'s Big Three.

—*Nine-Headed Dragon*—

Chapter 7 (**Feelings Taken Shape** Magical★Explorer)

For the past few days, people had been telling me that my head was in the clouds, and I was starting to think they had a point.

My dungeon challenge was almost upon me, yet I still couldn't take my mind off that dragon.

Since witnessing Yukine's display of martial prowess, it would play back in my mind at every opportunity. It had even affected my own practice swings, earning tepid glances from Yukine herself.

I'd spent day after day dreamily recalling the impressive flashes of her naginata. After several days of this, it seemed Yukine could overlook it no longer. She invited me to meet with her once classes were over.

I had preparations to make for my dungeon trip, so I had planned on coming to campus anyway.

"Man, it's been a while since I've come to school, and they're still glaring."

I was drawing everyone's attention.

"If it was fawning girlish cheers and starry-eyed looks of admiration, then maybe I wouldn't mind…"

"Put your mind at ease, Master. I've made sure to block out any and all high-pitched or shrill voices you might overhear."

"Except now that means you've gotten rid of the ones I wanted to hear the most."

"Not at all. In truth, I do not sense any such cheers you described in our vicinity. I thought you'd be hurt if I told you this, so I lied about the sounds I was blocking on purpose."

"And basically ejected even the smallest speck of hope from my head with it, huh?"

Oh well, I knew that anyway. Such was reality.

"I think it simply best not to dwell on such thoughts, and instead indulge in a sense of superiority."

"A sense of what now?"

"Consider it for a moment, if you will. Who do you have serving by your side?"

I casually turned my eyes to Nanami. At this, she spun around on the spot and curtseyed in front of me.

"Yes, that is right, a maid to best all maids. What more could you ask for than a stunningly beautiful lady serving you to the fullest?"

I smiled despite myself.

"And at the very least, Miss Ludie, Miss Yukine, Miss Hatsumi, Miss Claris, and I know how much effort you put in. We're all rooting for your success."

"……Yup, you're right. That's more than enough."

She was ranking one of the people she mentioned very highly, but well, that only made me happier.

"Also your classmates, such as Miss Katarina, Mr. Iori, Mr. Orange are all on your side, too, Master."

"Y'know, it makes me real glad to hear that."

As we walked a bit farther, a head of bouncy pink hair came into view. Though we were on our way to meet up with Yukine, it was a face I hadn't seen in a while, so I decided to call out to her.

"Good afternoon, Ms. Ruija."

She instantly shuddered and slowly turned toward us.

"*Uh-oh.*"

The teacher wore a stiff, rigid grin on her face, which quickly deflated into a look of sadness, as if she'd dropped the act.

"U-um, what is it then? I, um, have done my best to mentally prepare myself…"

Prepare for what, now? As I stood at a loss for words, Ms. Ruija continued.

"It's, well, erm, my first time, so…"

"What superb mental resolve. Very well. I shall grant you permission to approach my master for today."

"And what exactly are you two bringing up all of a sudden?"

I was used to Nanami doing this, but could Ms. Ruija cool it with disclosing such personal stuff out of the blue? For starters, I already knew that was the case with all the heroines who popped up in the game. If I recall correctly, Ms. Ruija was like that because she'd gotten indecisive after finding out her first crush already had a boyfriend. I was sure that must've given her a serious shock, in a lot of different ways...... More than I could possibly imagine.

"Do not worry, Master. I perfectly understand what you wish to say. Leave everything to your maid Nanami here."

"That makes me even more worried."

She then put her hands up, as if to calm me down and keep me back, before stepping out in front of my teacher.

"Ms. Ruija, my master would like to slowly develop your relationship, and thus would first request he use your lap as a pillow."

"Huh, but, um... That much shouldn't be a problem......"

Was it really okay? There didn't seem to be anyone else around, so I wasn't about to refuse to offer!

"Um, er, Takioto...... I've never seen this girl before...," Ms. Ruija stated, examining Nanami with confusion.

Yeah, you know, I hadn't ever seen a girl dressed up in a maid outfit striding across campus, either. Though there were others decked out in kimonos and stuff. What the heck was with this school......?

"Ah, right, she just recently enrolled."

"Whaaat? Recently? I—I haven't heard anything about it, though..."

I'd gotten permission from the highest authority (Marino) to bring Nanami here, so it was fine. Probably. In the meantime, it seemed best to smoothly change the subject.

"I haven't seen you lately. How have things been since?"

Ms. Ruija instantly brightened up.

"Everything's been great. The debt collectors have stopped calling me, and I've gotten a bit more breathing room in my day-to-day life. Actually, I have something I'd like to ask you."

She clutched her pink hair as she fidgeted bashfully.

"What's that?"

"Um, well... I was wondering if I could have just a bit more allowance......?"

I could very much understand why Nanami's face twitched in response. Anyone would be surprised to hear a teacher ask a student to increase her pocket money, really.

"I don't mind, but what are planning on using it on?"

Currently Ms. Ruija was under an allowance system. Her salary from the Academy was deposited into my bank account instead of hers. From there, I'd deduct her debt repayment, utilities, and the like, then deposit only the money it was safe for her to use into her account. Whenever I would transfer the funds into her account online, I'd wonder how the hell I ended up in charge of all this in the first place.

"Umm, well, see, there's apparently this pillow that gives you a really, really good night's sleep, and right now, for just—"

"Aaaand, denied. Let's go, Nanami."

"Wait! Where are you going?!"

I honestly felt sorry she'd even bothered to ask.

"Please, just a little bit more! They said it's only available for a limited time!"

"Ah, yup, yup. A comfortable pillow. There are some cheap options, so that should do it. I'll send one to you later."

I could just order it online and have it shipped to her address.

"That won't work! I have to buy this pillow noooow!"

That sure sounded like something straight out of a scam artist's playbook!

"It absolutely will work. Besides, I gave you a pretty good chunk of change for your allowance, didn't I?"

Ms. Ruija stuck her tongue out of the side of her mouth while fiddling with her hair.

"This store said they had a really good comforter, so… I used it all…"

She was cute, but that didn't cut it.

"Get a refund."

I headed toward where I was meeting Yukine, trying to shake Ms. Ruija off me along the way. Yukine had already arrived and was staring at us in total bewilderment.

"Hey, Yukine, I'm sorry… Ran a little late."

"O-oh, uh, hi. I was early, that's all. You're right on time, but…"

Yukine was unsettled. Well, I understood why. But more importantly, just how much longer were you planning on clinging on to me, Ms. Ruija?! Even when I tried to beat her back with my stole, she hung on for dear life.

"Listen, Yukine, what exactly does this look like to you?"

"Like a wife who's been caught cheating is desperately clinging to her husband and pleading with him not to leave her."

A soap opera, then? This was absolutely going to be making the rounds tomorrow.

"I see, then if I do this, it should really add to the realism," Nanami said before grabbing me from the side Ms. Ruija wasn't attached to. She'd formed a picture-perfect scene of two women fighting over a man. I knew what was going on here. This was like *Ivory Album* or *Academy Days*.

Yup, this was a soap opera, all right. Brushing them both aside, I entrusted (pushed) Ms. Ruija to Nanami and bowed my head.

"Apologies. For all of that."

"N-no worries. It's a lot to process at once, but I'm fine."

I glanced over to Nanami and found her talking about something with Ms. Ruija. For some reason that escaped me, Nanami gave a wink to Yukine before going off somewhere with the teacher.

"Ahem."

Yukine cleared her throat to try restarting the conversation fresh. Then...

"N-now then, even with exams starting tomorrow, you're still going through with your challenge, right?"

Hmm? I was at a loss for a moment.

Aaah, so that was why she wanted to talk to me.

"Yes, I am. Though, I didn't really plan on telling anyone besides Nanami and Marino about this..."

Despite emphasizing to Marino that I wanted her to keep it to herself so no one else would worry, she'd gone and told everyone about it the very next dang day...

"I see. *Ha-ha.* You're really going for it, then."

"I sure am. Part of my reason for coming to campus today was to prepare for it."

I had gotten my hands on everything I wanted. And when I thought back to what I'd needed to do before challenging the Tsukuyomi Academy Dungeon...I'd completed almost all of it.

"*Ha-ha-ha-ha!*" Yukine laughed, finding my reply deeply comical.

"At this point, I've gone far past sheer amazement at your unconventional way of doing things, so now I can't help but to laugh and respect it... That, and..."

Yukine took a green purse out of her school uniform pocket, then pulled something out of it. She walked up to where I was standing.

When she was one step away from me, she brushed aside her beautiful raven hair, slightly embarrassed, and tucked it behind her ear. Her porcelain, radiant cheeks and her crescent-shaped ears were exposed to the air.

Then she looked toward me with her gentle eyes, as if gazing at a newborn fawn, and giggled.

"Give me your hand."

When I extended my palm, Yukine placed the something from her purse in it. She then gently folded it closed with both of her hands.

"You talk about it like it's no big deal, but what you're trying to do is completely unorthodox and extremely difficult."

"Hmm, you really think so?"

"See what I mean? Just a day left, and you're still being glib. The dungeon is unforgiving. What you're attempting to accomplish is going to be more grueling than you could possibly imagine."

"Okay, okay, hold on. I do actually think it's going to be tough. Yet at the same time, I also think, 'Eh, I can handle it.' Part of me also believes that I'm never going to become the strongest if I can't get through this much."

It was going definitely going to be a rough time. The latter half of the dungeon especially.

"'This much,' huh? I could probably manage only the combat aspect, but in the time frame you're shooting for, it's just impossible. Only Student Council President Monica *might* be able to pull it off. It's just that hard."

The smile on Yukine's face disappeared, and she fixed me with a solemn look.

"To be honest, I want to go with you, too. I'd like you to bring me along with you."

Nobody wanted to bring her along more than me. Yukine, Ludie, Nanami, too. I wanted to tag along with them all. But I needed to go it alone, just this once.

"C'mon now, don't give me that look. You're doing this for a reason, right? I get it."

Yukine slowly took her hands from mine, as though reluctant to let me go. Sitting in the palm of my hand was a protective charm, with familiar scenery sewn onto its surface.

Sewn into the charm was a picture of a small waterfall and the stream below. That picturesque landscape.

The waterfall where we'd first met.

It was on private land. There were likely only a handful of people who even knew it existed, and even fewer who'd actually visited it. That was to say, this thing definitely wasn't sold in stores.

It was a handmade protection charm.

"You've given me all sorts of things," Yukine said, before stroking the ring on her finger. "Objects, emotions. Compared to this band you gave me, something like that isn't worth anything at all."

A bashful smile came to her face. I squeezed down hard on the charm.

"Yukine… That's not true. If I had to choose between those five rings and this protective charm, I'd chuck them into a volcano without a second thought."

That piece of jewelry she wore might have fetched quite a price. But to me, this protective charm that she'd sacrificed her precious pre-exam time to make for me was far more valuable.

"*Ha-ha*, that'd be a huge waste, dummy. But thank you."

I slowly opened up my hand and stared at her gift.

"Exams are right around the corner, and this is how you spent your time…? And that's on top of the time you've spent helping me out with my training, so who's the real dummy here? I couldn't be any happier."

This charm was quite intricately made. She couldn't have wrapped it up in an hour or two, that's for sure. During this vital reading period, not only had she joined me on dungeon runs and trained with me, she'd put in the time and effort to make this, too.

"Takioto…… I'm praying for your success."

The very first thing I thought upon meeting back up with Nanami was that she must've known about this.

She'd been aware of what Yukine planned to do, so she had steered Ms. Ruija away for me. That maid was almost too tactful, seriously.

"Hey, Nanami."

Which was why I decided to say it first.

"Thanks."

"Whatever could you be referring to, Master? Oh yes, you must be thanking me for recording my voice to use with the alarm clock app on your Tsukuyomi Traveler."

"Well, that would explain why it sounded so bizarre this morning."

She'd had the gall to record herself making lewd, aroused noises on that thing. Fortunately, I'd been half-asleep when it went off, so I was able to silence it without much thought, but if that had happened during my waking hours, I might not have been able to keep my cool.

"Absolutely not what I meant. You dragged Ms. Ruija away with you, right?"

"Yes, yes I did........."

Nanami suddenly had a faraway look in her eyes. She sighed quietly.

"It was a close battle. Any later, and that pillow would be well on its way to her apartment."

"Thank you for that, seriously. Must've been rough."

I couldn't begin to imagine what she'd gone through... I needed to change Ms. Ruija's phone number later......

Anyway, setting that aside for the moment...

"That's not what I meant, either. You knew, right? What Yukine was trying to do, I mean."

"Ah, that," she mumbled, as if resigning herself, before she dispassionately began to answer.

"If you're asking whether or not I did indeed know, then yes, I did. However, I didn't know she would do this today."

Which meant she must've figured it out when they'd exchanged looks with each other.

"...Master, please forgive me, but could you give me some of your time?"

She didn't need to ask for any forgiveness at all. For Nanami, I'd set aside all the time in the world.

We continued on into a spatial magic circle.

The Tsukuyomi Academy campus was unbelievably vast. In addition to the main buildings, there were a number of separate gym-like training areas, research labs, and entrances to various dungeons on the grounds. It was possible to teleport to any of them via spatial magic circles, but there were also a number of places devoid of people.

We were transported to one such area. After taking a seat on one of the many available benches, I gazed over the garden that spread out before me. In actuality, there was also a boy and girl who looked like a couple here, but our voices wouldn't reach them from where we were, so they probably wouldn't pay attention to us.

"This is a pretty nice place, isn't it?"

Nanami nodded.

"I largely agree. However, being so exposed to sniper fire puts us at quite the disadvantage…"

"Are we on a battlefield or something? When did this place get so dangerous?"

There was little in the way of cover in this place. The better question was, where exactly *wouldn't* we be exposed to sniper fire?

"Do not fear. With my skills, I'll be able to neutralize the target before they can get a shot off."

"You're the one who needs to be neutralized. No one's gonna shoot at us."

Obviously, this campus wasn't sketchy or dangerous… Right?

"Save the jokes for later. Let's get to the topic at hand, okay?"

At my words, Nanami mumbled with agreement.

"I suppose, if I have no other choice."

"Aren't you the one who invited me out here in the first place?"

"A joke, of course. Yes, obviously a joke. However, with your sharp intellect, Master, I imagine you already know what I wish to converse about."

Despite Nanami's confidence, there had been a lot going on lately, so I hadn't the slightest idea what she could be referring to.

"…In that case, allow me to give you a hint. The key words would be 'Master' and 'Reckless.'"

"Hmmm…… Is that supposed to be about tomorrow?"

I'd headed to the school store today to purchase the items I would need for my Tsukuyomi Academy Dungeon challenge tomorrow. Nanami went along to help me with my shopping, of course. Along the way, we'd discussed my upcoming dungeon outing a bit.

Taking all that into account, that was where my mind would go.

"Astute as always, Master. Your guess is right on the mark. Breakfast tomorrow shall be a Nanami full course."

"Yeah, I'd say that was a couple miles off the mark."

What in the world was she getting at here?

"That, too, was a jape, of course. You were absolutely right—I am referring to your dungeon trip," Nanami said, following it up with a small sigh.

"Normally, I would prefer to force you to bring me along, but… I will acquiesce just this once. However, since you'll be on your own, I imagine you will be gripped with abrupt bouts of loneliness. As such, I was left with little choice. Please, accept this."

Nanami slipped a hand into her cleavage and fished something out.

The face I made might not have been fit to be seen in public. I took the item, which had quite literally been warmed to body temperature, and stared at it.

Nanami had given me a protective charm.

There, drawn on its surface, was a maid in an excessively long scarf. "Master Kousuke Takioto is not complete without his maid Nanami."

Oh right, that explained the illustration.

"Miss Yukine informed me she had made a charm, so I made one of my own. Would you like to equip it now?"

"*Pfft!* What's with that phrase? Are we in a video game?"

"Equipping it will increase all your stats, you know."

"So we *are* talking video games, then."

I couldn't hold back my smile.

"Gah, sheesh... This makes me so dang happy, probably more than you could ever imagine."

I gently gripped her gift in my hand and held it up close to my chest. Nanami had gone and made something this intricate and time-consuming, too...

"Obviously, I'm gonna equip it immediately. You'd better be ready, because I'm not taking it off for the rest of my life, either."

At this, she looked taken aback. She widened her eyes.

"Um, it's, well...I did not expect it to make you so pleased. But, hearing you say that..."

She gave a warm smile.

"Makes me extremely happy, too."

As I stared at the maid's tender smile, I couldn't help but be spellbound. Once again, it struck me that Nanami really was an angel after all. Of course, the realization wasn't just in regard to her species, either.

"Listen, Nanami. Once I'm done clearing this dungeon, there are a whole bunch of other labyrinths I want to go to."

I trailed off and fixed my gaze on Nanami. She stared back with her heterochromatic eyes, unblinking.

"Will you come with me?"

"Your phrasing...is off," she replied, shaking her head.

"The thing to say isn't 'Will you come with me.' It is 'Come along with me.' I would join you wherever you go and wish to hear you say as much."

"……Got it. Then, come along with me, Nanami."

"As you wish, Master."

I wondered when it was, exactly, that I started to feel restless when I didn't get ready for things well in advance. When I'd been in elementary school, I didn't have any problem saving things until the last minute. In middle school, I'd always leave my textbooks and dictionary behind, so the inside of my backpack was usually filled with manga, snacks, and games. It must have been after transitioning to adulthood that I really started to make sure I was thoroughly prepared for things ahead of time.

"That should be just about it."

The only thing I needed now was food. My item box, which had gotten neither heavier nor bulkier when filled up with all my belongings, was beyond amazing—it was downright disgusting. It didn't just reinvent logistics, it revolutionized them. The only issue was that a high-performance item like this commanded an eye-poppingly high price tag.

In the game you have to seriously save to purchase it, yet in this world, one "Please?" to Marino had been enough to get my hands on it. There was seriously something screwy with this family's attitude toward money.

I had just finished placing my bags on top of my desk when there came three small knocks on the entrance to my room. "Come in," I called out. Ludie opened the door and stepped inside.

Though this was my room, she was already well-acquainted with it. No sooner had she gotten through the door than she'd sat down on my bed and placed Marianne, the stuffed orca that served as both my room's guardian deity and my full-body pillow, on top of her lap. She hugged it tight with both her arms.

Hey, Marianne? How'd that feel? Like heaven? Could you describe it to me? Or better yet, swap places with me?

"So tomorrow's the start of exams, right?"

"Yup, sure is."

"You're really going, then?"

"Of course. Especially after all this prep work I've put in."

I'd gone through a unique training regime for my forty-layer challenge and had gathered a slew of different items, too. In fact, those preparations were why I had even visited school today in the first place. Though meeting with Yukine had been another factor.

"Hmmm. I see. You are, then…," she replied as she grabbed on to Marianne's pectoral fin and flapped it back and forth.

"Are you leaving early in the morning tomorrow?"

"Nah, I'm planning on getting a slower start on purpose. I'll probably head out after I've triple-checked that I've got everything."

"I see."

"…Hey, so what's up, Ludie?"

She was acting a bit off today.

"… I've been causing you nothing but problems recently, haven't I?"

"Have you?"

I couldn't remember a single example.

"Yes," she responded, grabbing Marianne's dorsal fin and placing her on her lap. I wanted Ludie to let me use her lap as a pillow, too. "See, when you asked me for help and we went to that dungeon together, it made me kinda happy. I thought that maybe I managed to pay you back, just a little bit."

Then she added quietly, "Though there were some embarrassing moments, too," before she propped Marianne up and hid her face.

Oh yes, that dungeon. And those panties…… *Ahem.*

"Stop thinking about it!"

"S-sorry."

"…So then, when we managed to clear the ruins, there was this idiot who distributed all the most valuable treasure to the four of us. I tried to pay him back, but instead he foolishly gave it all back again."

Poking half her face out from behind Marianne, Ludie glared at me in reproach.

"That wasn't stupid. It was a logical conclusion. If there's someone else who can get more use out of something than I can, then they should be the one using it."

"But that doesn't mean you needed to outright give them away," Ludie said, shifting her eyes down. The ring in question was snugly fitted on her right hand.

"I wanted to give them to you all. I don't regret it one bit. You seemed like you'd put it to good use, but more than that, the color green really suits you."

"Geez...!"

Her cheeks flushed a light pink, Ludie threw Marianne at me. I caught the plushie and rubbed Marianne's still-warm face as I sat down beside Ludie.

"......Hey, Kousuke? Do you not need me around at all?"

"Where'd that come from...? I absolutely do."

"Even in the Tsukuyomi Academy Dungeon?"

"......I've got something that I have to do by myself, no matter what. So just this once, I want you to let me fly solo. Thing is, though, clearing the levels after that is gonna be totally impossible on my own."

On a second playthrough, Iori, Prez, and Yukine could manage it with relative ease. But that was probably too much for my finicky abilities. All the more reason why...

"So, when that time comes, will you come with me?"

"Of course I will..."

Ludie put her hand into her pocket, elbowing me a bit as she did.

"Kousuke, your hand."

"Hmm?

"Gimme your hand."

Letting go of Marianne, I held out my palm before Ludie. When I did, she placed something on top of it.

It was a protective charm, shaped similarly to Yukine's. Embroidered onto the simple fabric was a four-leaf clover.

"I heard from Yukine that she was giving you a Wakoku protection charm, and well... Nanami and I both had her teach us how to make them."

"...That explains why Yukine's been coming over here so often lately."

I'd *thought* the frequency of her visits had spiked dramatically. She'd been coming over once every three days. That guest room here was turning into her own. Though honestly, I was happy to have her around. She was a huge help with my training.

"Sorry, mine's not nearly as well-made as Nanami's and Yukine's, right?"

Hearing this, I gazed down at the charm.

"...I'll admit that it doesn't quite stack up to Yukine's, but how well it's made doesn't matter one bit. These keepsakes are all equally precious to me, impossible to judge against one another. Thank you."

Anything that Ludie had made by hand out of concern for me was an invaluable treasure.

"Okay......"

There was a moment of silence after her reply, until finally...

"Argh, honestly. Why are you insisting on going alone, anyway...?" she grumbled.

"It's just this once. I promise."

"I know. But still, I can't stand it. Gaaah! This really better be the last time you go off on your own."

"I know. I'll be sure to invite you along next time."

I couldn't suppress a wry grin when I saw Ludie huff. It looked like she was still annoyed with me. But I needed her to understand this.

"...Hey, Kousuke, stand up and turn around for a moment."

Hmm? Why? I thought, but despite my confusion, I obeyed and turned my back to Ludie.

Right after I did, I felt something warm and soft press up against my back.

Ludie was hugging me from behind. Her delicate hands were wrapped around my stomach, squeezing it tight.

"...Kousuke."

"What?"

"I heard there's a new ramen place near the station...... You're buying."

"Oh, sure. You got it."

If that was enough to wash away her anger, then it was a cheap price to pay.

I placed my hands atop hers, and she wrapped hers around mine.

"......Kousuke."

"What?"

"Good luck."

"......Thanks."

Tsukuyomi Academy Dungeon opened the day exams started—today. The written exams took four days, and the practical exams took one, so the testing period was five days in total. Following that was another two days to tally up all the scores. This came out to seven days total. Then scores would be posted on the eighth and final day.

If I wanted to take the top spot in the class, I needed to fully clear forty layers of the Tsukuyomi Academy Dungeon in about a week, starting today. Marino had also given me her word that, while it would be cutting it close, I'd secure the highest rank if I could finish my challenge by early morning on the eighth day. By the way, simply finishing the first twenty layers was enough to easily grab the top spot.

Now, in the *Magical★Explorer* game, you should be able to clear forty floors in four days with just Iori alone, even when fighting most of the monsters that show up. Provided you're using a new game plus Iori or an RTA speedrun Iori, that is. Kousuke Takioto certainly isn't up to snuff.

With that in mind, my current goal was six days. Not seven—six. That way, I could avoid running up against the limit and have a bit of breathing room.

If I was able to conquer forty floors in that time period, I would be able to grab the top rank in my class.

But even if the challenge took longer than the allotted seven days, I needed to keep aiming for the fortieth layer. No going back. The benefits I'd gain from clearing forty layers on my first trip were just that substantial. The only caveat was that I'd no longer claim top rank in my class in that situation.

And achieving the highest rank did have its perks.

One was receiving Tsukuyomi Points and special items.

If things in this world lined up with the game, then scoring well on exams allowed you to earn some pretty good items from the Academy. Additionally, you'd be rewarded with a large amount of Tsukuyomi Points.

Personally, however, those items and points were practically table scraps compared to one of the other rewards.

The second benefit was admission into one of the Three Committees (the Student Council, Morals Committee, or Ceremonial Committee). Taking the top score on these first exams was your quickest route to Committee membership. When that happens in the game, they approach the player about joining... They'd come talk to me about it in this world, too, right? Right?

Joining the Three Committees was extremely important. On top of making progress with various different events, I'd get the ability to go and challenge a certain dungeon. Most important of all, I'd have chances to interact with the other members of each Committee. That being said, most of the events were way down the line, and I planned on having Iori handle most of them. But if he ended up having a rough time, I was also willing to help him out... And if he *asked* me to, well, um... I—I guess I would want to lend him a hand. Maybe.

However, even admission into the Three Committees paled in comparison to the special bonus for clearing these layers on your first visit.

And what else could it be but a high-rarity item? After all, it wasn't first-time players, but those on their second playthrough who set their sights on it.

Sending a nearby carplin flying with a punch, I continued on through the maze without looking back to confirm if it was dead.

The finish line for the second layer was already in front of me. I only ever visited this level once per playthrough, so my memory of it had been foggy. To my surprise, however, I managed to get through it just fine.

"Already at the next level? I'm making good time."

Since I'd set everything up with Marino ahead of time, no one had tried to stop me when I came to challenge the Tsukuyomi Academy Dungeon. As of this moment, the map was exactly how I remembered it. Smooth sailing.

"The next thing to worry about...is this upcoming layer."

Maps were one of the variables that could cause me to fail to get through the forty floors. If the layouts were exactly how I remembered them, I could go from layer to layer via the shortest possible routes and drastically reduce my clear time. Conversely, if the maps differed even slightly from their in-game counterparts, or I forgot any of them, I'd need to be prepared to spend extra time running around the dungeon, lost.

Currently, everything in the dungeon was as I remembered. But the magic circle taking me to the next floor—which I had just entered—would determine whether that held true.

When I stepped out of the device, I found myself in a room constructed from brick, resembling the previous layer. I immediately broke into a run and continued through the wide hallways, big enough to fit seven to eight people across.

Then, I found the thing I was looking for.

"Awwwwww yeah! Oh, yes, yes, yes! It's a goblin; fan-*tastic*! I love you, little guy."

"*G-gobu?*"

Whether taken aback by my sudden confession of love, or because I had flown in out of nowhere, the creature was totally bewildered. I delivered a full-power gut punch with my Third Hand to send it flying and trampled over its body as I continued onward.

I was so elated, I'd ended up professing my love for a dang goblin. It looked like the monsters showing up were in line with what I remembered.

Now that my biggest worry, whether the encounters were the same, was gone...

"I'll just sprint on through the first ten layers."

Enemies? Weak. Experience points? Miniscule. Item drops? Garbage. Treasure chests? Didn't know if there were any and didn't care if there were. So what exactly *was* I supposed to do for this group of floors?

Simple. I needed to ignore all the enemies until I reached the boss on the tenth layer.

"At this rate, I should be able to clear ten floors on the first day...... And I'll be able to get plenty of sleep, too. Heck, maybe I should just press my advantage and keep going?"

Thinking while I ran along, I spotted a goblin looking my way.

He was raring to take me on, but since he was off in the distance, I ignored him and continued forward.

"Phew, I'm beat...... But I made it to the tenth layer......!"

The boss here was another one of the brown-leafed Wood Golems I had fought before. It might have posed a challenge a few weeks back, but it was now basically just a big scarecrow. I finished it off before it could put up a fight. Didn't even have to exploit its fire weakness with a magic sigil stone.

If anything, the long-distance running I'd been doing was more of a challenge than the boss at the end. I hadn't expected *this* would be where my daily running regimen bore fruit. That was supposed to be just for building up my stamina...

I still had some of my first day left over. But beyond this level, there wouldn't be any monster-free safe zones for a while.

Should I keep going deeper?

Nah. I decided to stop things here. I'd scheduled in a lot of breathing room for the first day of my trek. If I rushed ahead and ended up making a mistake that forced me to flee the dungeon, my whole plan to clear the first forty levels would fall apart.

That was the one thing I wanted to avoid at all costs.

"If this was an RTA speedrun that I could just reset, I'd totally charge forward, though."

I started getting my bed together. Though really it was nothing more than a simple sleeping bag.

According to what I was told, while there had been cases of people camping out for a day in the Tsukuyomi Academy Dungeon, no one had ever slept inside for a whole week. Well, that was only natural, really. Why the heck would you insist on snoozing inside the dungeon when there was a spatial magic circle every ten layers that teleported you back to the entrance? There was no question I'd rather be going to sleep back in my bed together with Marianne...... Though lately, I was finding either Sis or Nanami in bed with me when I woke up, instead. Oh boy, did that spook me.

If I stayed in the dungeon for six to seven days, would people start saying I owned the place? Nah, I doubt a mere week was enough for that.

My simple bedding was good to go. Next up: Food. I'd skipped lunch to keep running, so it made sense that my stomach was growling up a storm. I needed to eat well, sleep well, and maintain my energy for the days ahead.

I took out the meals Sis and Nanami had prepared for me.

Nanami had handed me hers and said, "D-don't get the wrong idea or anything, I made this specifically for you, Master." I'd had no clue how to respond. Conversely, the only thing Sis uttered was "Hrm." The two of them had gotten up bright and early to make them for me.

Both of the lunchboxes contained sandwiches.

They must've been considerate enough to go with sandwiches, assuming that I'd actually eat them for lunch, so I could scarf them down on the go. But since I wasn't hungry earlier, I'd reserved them for dinner.

I picked up the lunchbox filled with a humble and very tasty-looking egg sandwich. This was the lunch Nanami packed for me.

She'd carefully calculated when to take the eggs off the boil, cut them into quarters to reveal perfectly runny orange yolks, and covered them with egg salad. Then she'd wrapped it all up with crispy-looking pieces of lettuce before placing them between some bread. A truly gorgeous egg sandwich. It looked absolutely delicious!

Now in a cheery mood, I opened up the lunchbox Sis had given me.

I immediately lurched back.

They looked, well, edible, at least.

Inside were a few uncomplicated spicy sandwiches, stuffed with crisp lettuce that had been doused in a harsh crimson chili sauce. Or at least that's how they *looked*.

While I hadn't tasted them yet and could only take my best guess, this didn't seem to be as straightforward and simple a sauce as it appeared. Timidly, I brought the sandwich up to my face.

No, this couldn't be possible...... Why?

Why was there such an intense energy-drink smell coming out of this thing? I didn't have the slightest clue. This wasn't the smell of a spicy hot sauce. This definitely reeked of energy drink. For the time being, I picked up one of Nanami's egg salad sandwiches.

"Yup. Delicious."

The fluffy egg salad, perfectly salty runny egg, and fresh vegetables came together inside my mouth to create a wonderful harmony that nearly moved me to tears. I picked up one more, and then another, and it wasn't long before they were all gone.

I took a deep breath. Then I turned my eyes toward the unfathomable sandwiches that continued radiating their intense energy-drink stench.

If there was a choice box displayed in front of me, the three options would be EAT, DIG IN, and CHOW DOWN. An ABSTAIN option wouldn't be available.

Despite how terrible she was at getting up, Sis had miraculously woken up early in the morning to make these for me. I was obviously going to eat them. Of course I would…eat them…

With a trembling hand, I grabbed one of the sandwiches. Compared to Nanami's, the bread was oddly soft.

It wasn't that they *looked* bad. Normally, I would've described it as a very tasty-looking hot sauce. But *oof*, that energy-drink stench. The gap between the smell and their appearance horrified me.

The gap…the gap. Why was I so terrified of it?

If a rough-and-tough delinquent girl was actually really easily embarrassed and bashful at home, would that gap discourage me? If a normally dignified and dependable big-sister character turned in a marshmallow-like, fawning, and unreliable blob when it came to romantic relationships, would that gap turn me off?

It was the exact same with this sandwich.

As for what specifically was the same in this instance, I hadn't the faintest idea, but I had to think like that to keep myself going.

Steeling myself, I dug into Sis's creation.

What a truly sublime morning. I was in a stuffy dungeon with no sky or windows, yet despite that, why did I feel so refreshed?

I glanced down and found my garments in disarray, as if I had been attacked by something. My clothes were undone and my chest fully bared, with everywhere else in various states of tatters. I looked quite like heartthrob actors on magazine covers, who wore their outfits in a state of sexy dishevelment.

As I adjusted my outfit, I looked around and saw two empty lunchboxes sitting beside me.

What the heck is in these? I wondered. There was a nebulous energy-drink stench lingering in one of the boxes.

I checked the time on my stopwatch and clock app and let out a small sigh.

What exactly happened yesterday?

The only thing I could say for certain was that I felt like all of my exhaustion had been wiped away. And for some strange reason, it felt like I was overflowing with vim and vigor.

I couldn't remember anything at all, but I figured it didn't matter either way.

All right then, it was about time to get moving. Today's goal was to get to the twentieth layer! I needed to maintain this enthusiasm and rush through in one big burst of energy! This was the only time I'd really be able to charge through the dungeon.

Because after the twentieth layer, things were going to get real hard, real fast...

I didn't think that the journey from the tenth layer to the twentieth would be too difficult. The monsters here were as strong as the ones that showed up in the panties dungeon and the turtle-farming dungeon. However, starting from the eleventh layer, there was one part that was impossible to avoid and required some degree of strategy. That was...

"Didn't take me long to find one... I knew this ring from the Gloomy Ruins would come in handy."

I hopped over the trap in front of me, then took a nearby rock and threw it inside. When I did, something slid into place with a *clank* before wooden logs appeared out of the wall beside the trap and passed through the other side before my eyes. As if there were no walls at all.

It was a clearly a supernatural phenomenon, the kind that was inconceivable back on Earth. But according to Nanami, this was totally normal. I needed to keep in mind that the traps in the dungeons were just as abnormal as everything else in them.

I placed my hands on the weathered ring.

This thing was so valuable that I'd prepared myself to degrade my reputation to obtain it. Without it, soloing the first forty levels would've been an unrealistic fantasy.

Unfortunately, this ring would only have an effect for the first forty layers. Intermediate traps started popping up after that, which were too much for it. For this trip, I was only progressing up to the fortieth layer, so I'd be able to get by, but I'd need Nanami to work hard for me going

forward. Though part of me still wanted to trigger the erotic traps, too…
What a contradictory conundrum.

The monsters that started showing up after the tenth layer were completely different from the ones that had appeared on the first ten. Those monsters would be totally swapped out by around the fifteenth layer, but until then, there was one variety that was a real hassle to deal with. And it had just appeared before me.

The creature had a head like a dog's.

Its tongue dangled from its open mouth, which was lined with sharp fangs. It also carried a club, the sort a Neanderthal might wield, but considering how gangly the monster looked, it didn't seem like a blow from it would hurt very much.

This was my first time seeing it in this world, but it was a staple enemy in almost any fantasy game—a kobold. They were generally treated as trash mob enemies, and *Magical★Explorer* was no exception.

So what about them was a hassle, exactly? Their speed.

They were fairly agile. Kobolds had poured their stats into agility over strength. Defeating them was easy. I would defend their incoming attacks with my Third Hand and use that opening to either punch them with my Fourth, or finish them off with my katana's iai. While they were fast, their speed wasn't remotely comparable to Yukine's or Claris's.

But when you were planning on running away from them, everything changed.

Since kobolds had good hearing and astute scent-tracking skills, and were reasonably quick on their feet, they were quite difficult to escape from. That didn't mean it wasn't worth going out of my way to kill them all, though……

The kobold in front of me readied its club and watched my movements carefully.

These monsters are intelligent and won't attack you blindly. Instead, they wait for an opening to go on the offensive. Sometimes they'll even flee when you attack them. But after you are sure they have turned tail, they will come up from behind to ambush you, among other nasty tactics.

Quite the crafty little monsters.

To be honest, this was my first time coming across one. Most of what I knew was secondhand knowledge from Yukine, so I wasn't sure about the attacks from behind and so on. Still, I was taking everything she told me at face value.

That aside, just how long was this guy going to stand there watching me for an opening?

This staredown was simply a waste of my time. I abruptly put my hand in my pocket to grab one of my sigil stones and filled it with mana. Then I chucked it toward the kobold.

The beast dodged it easily. However, since I'd transferred my mana into it, the sigil stone activated as it passed right by it.

"_____!"

A shrill sound enveloped the area.

I sent my Third Hand flying into the kobold as it held down its large dog ears, ignoring the magic stone and particles to continue on.

Wonderful. The sound sigil stone had worked beautifully. While it was one of the cheaper varieties of low-level sigil stones, its effects were outstanding. Depending on how it was used, it had more versatility than the basic elemental sigil stones of fire, water, wind, and earth.

They were so effective, they helped me come out on top against Claris once. She came up with a way to counter it and beat me to a pulp afterward, though.

"These sigil stones are really handy, but..."

Useful and effective. But costly. While they were on the cheaper end, sigil stones themselves still commanded quite a price, so it had been a significant sum overall. As I progressed further, I'd start needing other types of sigil stones, too. Unfortunately, I wasn't able to carry as many as I would have liked.

If I hadn't been born into a family that bought imported sports cars as a sixteenth-birthday present, I would've either needed to give up on my solo forty-layer challenge or put my turtle farming on hold to raise funds. God bless Queen Marino.

There were only going to be more troublesome enemies popping up from here on out, as well as stronger foes in general, so I was going to be bleeding money from every orifice as I continued on. When I finished clearing this dungeon, though, I'd get an item that would make me forget all about the money I'd hemorrhaged, and the Three Committees' invitation should trigger as well. My wallet would be in real trouble if I failed. Not nearly as bad as a certain teacher I knew, though.

Finishing my sprint through the eleventh layer, I headed to the next. Naturally, I planned on dashing through this one, too.

I'd resolved to cut out any combat between layers eleven to twenty, too, to save time. That wasn't a personal preference, either; I estimated that I wouldn't make it to the fortieth layer in time otherwise.

Assuming I did fight between layers eleven and twenty along the way, the most annoying enemy of all were the bloody bats that started appearing on the thirteenth layer. As their name suggested, they were red, bloodsucking bat monsters. They tended to show up in large groups and were always hovering in the air, which made them irritating to fight. Yukine had told me that in her experience, they appeared in groups about 80 percent of the time.

If Ludie was with me, she could've used magic to knock them down. Similarly, if Nanami was here, she could blow them out of the sky. Me, on the other hand? I was just a monkey throwing rocks. But it wasn't worth spending sigil stones to fight the bats, either. Killing them wasted precious time.

Thus, I concluded that I needed to run away from them. If I had just a little more time, I would've been fine clearing them out a little as I delved deeper underground.

Just then, I turned at a fork in the path and let out an involuntary *"ugh."* In front of me was a group of three kobolds. Three big pains in the ass, in other words.

I quickly shoved my hand into my pocket, took out a few sound sigil stones, and activated them. Casting a sidelong glance at the three monsters writhing in pain and gripping their ears, I resumed my sprint.

It was then that a thought suddenly crossed my mind:

Wait. Ever since entering this dungeon, I've pretty much run away from every single enemy outside of the boss fights, haven't I?

Wrapping up the first twenty floors in two days lined up perfectly with my schedule. Given that I'd focused exclusively on running away, it was an easily foreseeable outcome. The twentieth-layer boss, a pig bastard known as an orc, wasn't even worth mentioning. I mean for starters, any pig that didn't fly was just a regular old pig, and any piggy rascal without a bunny girl was just a plain old piggy rascal.

From there, I immediately ate dinner and turned in for the night right afterward, bringing the second day to a close.

I didn't wake up feeling as great as I had the day before. I stretched out my arms, threw back some coffee, and after psyching myself up with a "Layer twenty-one, here I come!" immediately embarked on my dungeon run for the day. The moment I'd been waiting for had finally arrived.

The atmosphere in the twenty-first layer was different from all the layers that came before it.

Put simply, the normal stonework dungeonscape had given way to an interior reminiscent of jungle ruins, with vegetation encroaching into the structure of the dungeon. Tree roots, moss, and the like were growing on the walls and ground. If I didn't watch my step, I could easily trip over them.

Though really, none of that mattered—my problem was with the thing in front of me.

It had finally showed its face. Since *Magical ★ Explorer* was indeed an eroge, I definitely wouldn't be able to slip past it.

Its body was small. About three feet tall. Flapping its tiny wings, it pointed its fork-like spear in my direction.

In certain respects, this type of monster was stronger than most of the bosses around this level. It was rare to see an eroge RPG without them; I doubt such a game even existed.

This monster, still staring me down, was dressed in an outfit very unsuited for the location.

A competition swimsuit.

I'd have no qualms if this were a pool. But this was a dungeon. The average person would take once glance at this monster and simply conclude it was a pervert. Though it was a pretty typical sight in an eroge.

Seriously, why the hell was it wearing a competition swimsuit in the middle of an underground labyrinth? On top of all that, the creature had a long, thin tail growing out from somewhere—it wasn't clear if it was coming out of its lower back, its butt, or somewhere in between— with a spade-shaped tip.

Perfectly plump thighs, suntanned skin, and a not-quite-fully-developed chest. All features of its superbly healthy body, which was neither too skinny nor too pudgy.

It was glaring at me, as if to declare that it was going to take me down, but I want to give my truly honest opinion on the monster:

She was absolutely adorable.

"*Whew*, so the sexy monsters are finally showing up. And a bit of a loli one at that."

The imps that began appearing in the twenty-first layer of the Tsukuyomi Academy Dungeon looked different from the imps that showed up in other games. Monsters that had been tweaked to be cuter and sexier often cropped up in eroge. And most surprising of all was that they were all at least eighteen years old, of course.

If I could befriend monsters, I'd get to know this one straightaway. Even if she was weak, I'd use any item I could to make her capable of standing up to the late-game bosses. Well, by then she'd probably have grown up and turned into a *very* sexy, older lady imp. Though, depending on how she was raised, the "Legal-Loli" option was always there, too.

In truth, up until now, I had avoided these types of creatures. Nanami aside, I had no idea how I should react to them in the presence of Yukine and Ludie. Hell, I didn't even know how I *would* react to them in the first place.

Although there were no imps in the dungeons I introduced to Iori, there should've been other types of erotic monsters that showed up in them. In fact, I'd told him about those mazes on purpose; I wonder how exactly he'd reacted in front of the other girls in his party?

I'd get him to spill all the details later for my sake. Forgive me for using you as my guinea pig, Iori. But surely, it helped you level up......

Well, I guess erotic monsters were a regular feature of this world, so who knows? He could be used to them already.

The imp girl looked ready to fly at me at any moment, but I knew exactly how to handle her.

"Here ya go!"

I shoved my hand in my pocket and threw a sound sigil stone at her that instant, then dashed away at full speed. What else was I supposed to do? Being attacked from the air was difficult enough, and her titillating and suggestive form made it harder to deal with.

For starters, I seriously doubted I'd be in any state to fight back, thanks to the deliciously synergistic combo of her midair position and suggestive costume design. If I fought her normally, it'd take all sorts of time. And totally tucker out my brain...... Though, maybe I should have snapped a photo before I ran off.

However, I couldn't exactly run from every single monster I encountered on this floor. If I didn't bring down a certain number of them, I'd run into an experience points deficit.

I understood from my turtle farming that collecting magic particles was an extremely important part of strengthening myself. Farming was the most surefire way of improving my physical body. Though, that didn't necessarily mean my running and practice-strike routines were totally meaningless, either.

I truly felt the results from my daily running, even when I was only using them to flee from everything. My sword-drawing arts would especially prove vital down the line.

"There you are."

In addition to its completely different environment, the twenty-first layer featured different monsters, too. This was as true for the imp I'd encountered earlier as it was for the treant that had just appeared in front me.

Treants are a species of creature similar to wood golems, except I'd say they are closer to actual trees. As for their distinguishing characteristics, they are a so-called power-type that boast high-attack in exchange for low speed. Since they're weak to fire, you can totally shut them down by putting some distance between yourself and them and using fire magic. Though it is possible to overpower them without it.

The treant slowly lumbered toward me, then it swung its branch arm down. As I blocked the blow, it dawned on me just how absurdly strong Yukine and Claris were, before I repelled the creature's limb. Then I instantly launched my Sword-Drawing Arts—Flash—into its exposed stomach.

Since it is mainly a physical-damage monster—and slow, to boot—treants are little more than wooden training dummies once you overpower them. I had plenty of methods at my disposal for taking them out.

I cleanly sliced the creature in two and got a glimpse at the treant's inner wood grain. As I casually thought to myself, *Oh, right, you can figure out a tree's age by counting its growth rings*, the treant dissolved into a magic stone and magic particles.

"These magic stones are getting bigger, too..."

The enchanted rocks dropped by monsters, which were smaller than pigeon feed in the upper layers of the dungeon, had now gotten as big as my pinky finger...... They were still pretty tiny, though. Oh well. According to Ms. Ruija, I didn't need to worry about their size very much due to things like "building blocks," "density," and "condensation of form," or whatever she'd been going on about.

My teacher was incredibly reliable at her job and with magic; just being near her cheered me up. If only she could do something about that terrible money habit of hers.

Treants were also pretty easy to farm, and if these versions were the same as their in-game counterparts, they should have a ton of mana. They dropped pretty valuable magic stones, too. I considered the possibility of farming them here and gathering magic particles before ultimately nixing the idea.

"Why do there have to be poisonous monsters here, too?"

I hadn't come across any yet, but poison toads also appear in the layers where treants show up. If I happened to slip up somehow and get myself poisoned, how would I heal myself?

Items were my only option, and fortunately, I had prepared a fair amount ahead of time. The poison from this layer was pretty weak, so you could treat it with cheap antidotes. Those were a lot easier to buy than magic sigil stones.

That being said, I hadn't brought that many with me. The sigil stones were so dang useful that I'd gone all-in on them instead.

"That was actually a big mistake on my part......"

Even if I didn't plan on fighting the toads, the argument could be made that I should get poisoned at least once. In the game, you can still level up when you're under poison's effects. Since the toxins that showed up on this current layer were weak and barely dealt any damage, some players felt it was just easier to grind without curing it.

I could try doing that myself, but the possibility that the poison could have other effects that weren't immediately apparent in the game had me anxious.

In the game, for instance, sprinting across the map at all times won't diminish your ability to fight in any way. But in this world, the faster and faster I hurried, the more exhausted I became. After running for a while, my breathing would get labored, and I'd experience other drawbacks that weren't present in the game.

Just what sort of drawbacks came with being poisoned in this world? I probably should have figured that out before it came time to jump into this dungeon.

My plan had been to ignore all the monsters besides the treants on this layer. But the possibility that I could get poisoned still remained. I should have tried experiencing that before coming here.

Was it a good idea to try that out now? Nah. I didn't know what might happen, so it was better to hold off. It would be safer to test it out with another person when I wasn't operating under a time limit.

I didn't know for sure, but I figured Sis or Ms. Ruija had some sort of poison on them. There was no question that Sexy Scientist did. Oh yeah, she absolutely did, I'd swear to the god of eroge on that. Though, it was terrifying to think about what she'd demand in return if I asked for her help.

I'd made my first mistake since coming down here.

Before diving into a dungeon, I'd needed test out everything I could ahead of time. I was going to be heading into plenty more in the future. I could capitalize on this error to make sure it didn't happen again.

There was nothing I could do to fix that in my current run, though. I'd just have to farm treants and flee from everything else.

For now, I needed to clean up the treant that had just showed up in front of me.

The most important element of leveling up, especially in online games, is time. The time it takes to finish a single battle, the time it takes to encounter a monster, the time you spend healing and prepping your characters after the conclusion of a fight. To level effectively in a game, you have to add that all together and head to the most time-efficient area. Though your farming spot of choice often changes when you take item drops into account.

But for speedruns, that paradigm shifts. Since you're focused solely on your route to the end of the game, you need to anticipate everything up to the credits, and consistently take the shortest methods of getting there.

My end-goal was conquering the first forty layers of the dungeon in a week, along with admission into the Three Committees.

Since I felt these goals should be prioritized above all else, I'd sunk almost all my money into preparing for my journey, and I had put myself through a unique training schedule to make that possible. Hell, I'd even offered up three girls' used panties to make it this far.

Collecting magic particles was one of the things I absolutely needed to accomplish over the course of my forty-layer challenge. *All those treants on the twenty-first layer mean I just have to farm them!* Or so I'd thought, but there had been poison toads there. *In that case, I'll farm them starting on the twenty-fourth layer, when the poison toads stop showing up!* was how I wished things would play out.

It was all too unfortunate, then, that the treants also stopped showing up after the twenty-fourth layer. The imps still continued to appear, though, and I couldn't help but praise the devs for their astute understanding of what the people wanted. If I was able to use long-ranged light magic, or the sort of long-ranged attacks at Nanami's disposal, then they would have been quite lucrative to farm. But I didn't have any of those skills. So if the imps flew up in the air, I'd have to rely on my sigil stones to down them, all while their costumes took a toll on my mind. I could always lure them into a corridor, but the time spent leading them there would go to waste.

"Ultimately, running away's the best choice, really……"

Hobgoblins, stronger versions of goblins that started appearing from this floor on, would carry clubs, swords, bows, and staffs. While their attack patterns changed depending on the weapon they carried, each version was easy to deal with since they were as weak and forgettable as their in-game counterparts.

But while they were easy to kill, to my dismay, they rewarded less experience than the treants. I should've expected as much since they were so weak.

The hobgoblin now standing before me was the bow-wielding kind. But Nanami's bow skills were on a completely different planet compared to this thing. Honestly, a hit from its arrows felt like a punch from a kindergartner. Meanwhile, Nanami's constant barrage of bolts induced nothing but pure terror.

When they appeared in a group, it was a bit more efficient to farm hobgoblins than treants, but they didn't always work together. And when too many of them gathered, accidents happened (messing up and taking damage).

I'd brought a large amount of healing items into the dungeon, but I expected to be using them up left and right after the thirtieth layer, so I didn't want to break into them just yet.

After beating the hobgoblin to a pulp, it was back to running. If there were less than three, I'd fight. If there were more than three, or an imp decided to tag along, I'd run away.

Hopefully, I could keep progressing like this and get to the twenty-seventh layer without a hitch.

"Never mind, looks like I'm already here."

It had happened in the blink of an eye. I'd rushed my way here a bit faster than I had with the other layers up until now. But that was understandable considering I'd wanted to get here ASAP.

The twenty-seventh layer of the dungeon was a very important one that would control how things would play out for the rest of my run. It was one of the floors where monster encounters swapped out. In my current state, it was also the best map for grinding experience points.

Another noteworthy feature of this floor—the environment shifted again here. Perhaps it was only appropriate that the monsters changed to suit the scenery.

"Except, I'm gonna have to keep my guard up against sneak attacks from here on out."

Starting with this layer, canals and ponds started cropping up amid the jungle ruins environment. As such, water-based monsters grew more frequent.

I headed farther into the twenty-seventh layer. Right as I came upon a large, pond-sized pool of water, it appeared.

My eyes were drawn to its colossal pincers. Along with the huge shell it bore on its back. And a pair of feelers. And yeah, it was big. Height-wise, it looked about as tall as a third or fourth grader, maybe? However, it was about six or seven people wide, and boasted freakishly huge pincers. Too huge, if anything. They threw the creature off balance.

"But that lack of balance is what really screams 'timreh,' huh?"

Timreh are enemies based off hermit crabs, but with extravagantly enlarged pincers. Since the name is simply the word *hermit* spelled backward, players can immediately figure out what they are based on. Official sources even refer to them as "hermit crabs" occasionally. Many of the terms in *Magical★Explorer* are just anagrams or words written backward.

I'd be hard-pressed to find a monster better suited for my fighting style than a timreh. They weren't that fast, and while they resisted slashing attacks, they were weak to blunt ones.

Not only that, but Yukine had told me, *"You can slice through their joints pretty easily. And with your skill, Takioto, I bet you could even cleave through parts of their shells, too,"* so I was probably fine. Now that I thought about it, swords dealt a decent amount of damage to them in-game, which must have represented their joints getting sliced up. At any rate, my best weapon was my stole, so I could simply bash it to a pulp without needing to force myself to cut it at all.

There was one thing I needed to be cautious about.

The timreh turned and started advancing toward me, making a grinding sound as it dragged its claws along. It was faster than I had thought it'd be.

The crustacean swung its pincers up before slamming them down at me. *Seriously, you're not even gonna grab me with them?* I thought to myself as I turned my Third Hand into a fist to deflect the blow.

I needed to be wary of the enormous claws on these things. While they weren't sharp enough to cut through everything, those rugged pincers boasted enough strength to snap me in two.

When I sent a full-powered kick to its claws with my powered-up legs, the crab bent far back. Without delay, I sent my Fourth Hand straight into its face.

The timreh flipped onto its back with a loud crack, like something breaking apart. I went for another strike because it didn't turn into particles, but that didn't work, either. Rather, I was denied.

Bubbles frothed up and overflowed from the timreh. Its face was immediately covered in bubbles, as if growing a bubbly beard on the spot.

This monster wasn't venomous, so I didn't think there'd be any problem getting soaked by them…

"But it's kinda hard to get in close……"

Why did it feel so gross to look at? Maybe it was because the bubbles were slimy, or because they were so many of them?

That said, I still needed to fight it. For one, I had planned on wrapping up all the layers from twenty-one to thirty besides this one in just a few hours, so I could stay here for a day or more.

I was going to spend a lot of time here, and all of it would be spent farming, so stalling just because they looked a little gross would be a waste of my precious time.

"All right, let's do this. One, two…"

I steeled myself and punched its face in. To my surprise, even more bubbles gushed out from its maw. Eventually, it began convulsing before its feet gave way with a jerk and its shell fell to the ground. Finally, it began to slowly dissolve into magic particles.

Hermit crabs seemed like they were saltwater animals, but maybe they could live in freshwater, too? I went to pick up the leftover magic stone as those meaningless, idle thoughts crossed my mind before immediately standing back up. I then kicked the magic stone on the ground away for the time being, making sure it wouldn't get in the way of the upcoming fight.

"Like a moth to a flame, huh?"

Before my eyes appeared a monster I would be spending a whole day in the twenty-seventh layer to farm.

It had the physique of a child and carried a massive hammer. Coupled with its androgynous facial features, it had an extremely charming appearance. However, the sight of it lugging its huge hammer, likely even bigger than I was, across the ground, was bizarre, without a doubt.

It was a type of fairy monster, a knocker.

Knockers had the outward appearance of a child, but their strength didn't match their looks in the slightest. More than anything else, that human-size hammer………wasn't the big problem.

"Right out of the damn gate?!"

I turned my Third Hand toward the magic circle that appeared in front of the knocker. Then, pumping in more mana than usual, I enchanted it with water.

At the same moment, the fireball that popped out of the magic circle came flying toward me.

The most annoying part about these fairies' behavior was the fire attacks they launched using sigil stones. Promptly repelling the orb of fire with my stole, I closed the distance between us. However, as though it had been waiting for me to do so, it swung its hammer toward me from the side. I guarded with my Fourth Hand and tried to use my katana iai, but it didn't work.

The knocker capitalized on the momentum from its swing to jump back away from me.

"What the hell?" I couldn't help but mutter. Was it an acrobat or something?

It was unbelievably flexible. If I uploaded a video of this to the Internet, it would absolutely go viral, especially because of its boyish appearance.

The instant after it put some distance between us, the fairy grabbed another sigil stone and activated it. At the same time, it readied its hammer and sent it at me.

How unfortunate.

I had asked Yukine, Ludie, as well as Claris, to help me practice against two-pronged attacks. I knew I'd end up being outnumbered a lot inside the dungeon, and training myself to deal with it as best as I could had clearly been the correct call.

Repelling the fireball with my Third Hand, I blocked the hammer with my Fourth. However, this time my Fourth Hand was slightly different from before.

The moment the hammer struck my stole, it made a *fwump* sound, as though it had hit loose fabric, and my Fourth Hand swallowed it up. Just how long did this thing think it had taken me to master subtly controlling my stole's rigidity like this?

"All right, now I'll beef up my enchantment, then harden my stole… There."

The knocker tugged on its hammer, now encased in hardened fabric and unable to be pulled out. It was wide open.

Using my katana's iai, I cleaved the fairy clean in two. It morphed into magic particles, a magic stone, and a single red gemstone. Looking at it, I couldn't hold my surprise.

"Huh? N-no way. What's going on? It doesn't make sense."

I reflexively did a double take. My bewilderment far outweighed my happiness.

I wasn't planning to spend a whole day farming knockers just for the experience points. If anything, they were hard to grind, and there were more efficient locations where I could have done so. Nevertheless, I'd intentionally camped out where I had because the knockers here dropped a lucrative item.

Unfortunately, it had quite a low drop rate. They were still higher than the gacha rates for crappy cell phone games, but at least with those, you could get what you wanted as long as you coughed up the cash.

But there was no pay-to-win option here.

That being said, you could technically purchase this item if you wanted. It was just so expensive that it even put my allowance (equivalent to the yearly take-home of a first-year office worker) to shame. I'd decided to leave it off my shopping list since I wouldn't have been able to buy anything else if I'd purchased it. If I didn't have to work so hard to earn this one item, I might've been able to shorten my dungeon dive by an extra day. Though, honestly, the Hanamuras seemed like they'd raise my allowance without a second thought if I pestered them enough.

Lying on the ground near the recently defeated knocker was a single magic stone.

When I streamed my RTA runs, everyone had declared me the "RNG fail lord," so I'd never expected this thing to drop off of the very first fairy I defeated. I mean, I was definitely happy about it, no doubt about that!

I picked it up and got a good look at it. Yeah, I was glad that I always carefully admired all the different items for sale. This was the same item that fetched a pretty penny in the shop, no question about it.

An intermediate fire sigil stone.

Still, it was strange. I had no idea why the knockers dropped intermediate sigil stones when all they used were lesser sigil stones. Well, they did drop the lesser ones, too. They should've gotten off their high horses and used their damn intermediate stones. No matter how their opponent may've looked, they shouldn't have let down their guard. Oh well, whatever.

"Welp, I got my hands on a magic sigil stone..." I remarked, putting away the magic stone from the timreh I had previously kicked away with the arrival of the knocker. I couldn't wipe the big grin off my face.

"Guess I'll farm 'em until I get four more!"

My (optimistic) target time was twelve hours. It was non-stop grinding until they showed up!

............And so my hell had begun.

Random probabilities will eventually converge...was something I stopped being able to declare with confidence at around hour number six. In the end, it took me about twelve hours, just like I'd originally estimated, before finally getting my hands on the magic sigil stones I wanted. But by that point, I was despondent.

I tried doing *something* to get my spirits back up, which ended up being a sprint all the way to the boss on the thirtieth layer.

From the twenty-eighth floor, the hobgoblins and friends disappeared, with perytons, flying monsters that looked like deer with bird wings, appearing in their place.

Naturally, I ran in the opposite direction of every one of them. However...

"It's starting to get tougher to fight and flee, too..."

That was partially because the monsters were getting stronger abilities and stats, speed included. But more than anything, they'd gotten a lot craftier.

The peryton that came rushing at me out of the sky while I wrapped up a knocker fight was a great example. I instantly defended against it with my Fourth Hand, but it was an extremely dangerous ambush.

On this floor, the knockers I'd spent hours farming sometimes wouldn't even bother chasing me at all. No sooner would this strike me as strange than I would run into a bear trap.

Although I was still on layers where the monsters were comparatively easy to deal with, I would be in bad shape from the thirty-first floor onward. From there, it would be nothing but monsters either at or above my level.

For now, I used a (lesser) light sigil stone on the peryton in front of me and made a hasty retreat.

"I'm watching money drain out of me like water...... Though I guess having too much left over at the end wouldn't be great, either."

Having too much leftover cash could only be considered a failure to properly predict what you needed for your adventure.

It signified that you hadn't done enough research beforehand.

But in my defense, I'd been barred from delving into the dungeon prior to the testing period. That was why I'd needed to anticipate what I would need based off my knowledge of the game and questions to Yukine. It really wasn't my fault I hadn't foreseen everything.

After using up my entire supply of light sigil stones, I arrived at the thirtieth layer. Like all of the other nice, round numbered levels, there was a boss waiting for me. No surprise there.

The floor was best described as an oval field. A bit like an athletics stadium, but with all the audience seating around it replaced with a water channel.

When I walked into the center of the floor, something in the canal in front of me made a splash.

A dark brown shell surfaced from the water and started to approach me.

The next thing to emerge was a large pincer.

But the claw on this creature wasn't the same as the ones belonging to the hermit crabs that I had just spent more than ten hours fighting over and over again. No, it was much larger—and much thicker—than that. On top of that, this boss's shell wasn't the characteristic shell of a hermit crab, but a carapace enveloping its whole body.

"There you are, Clammbon."

Clammbon was a monstrous crustacean.

Its appearance was totally, 100 percent crab, but its size was far beyond any normal crustacean's. Its pincer alone was big enough to easily lift me off the ground... Actually, it would've likely torn me instantly in two, it was so huge. As I watched the creature raise its massive pincers threateningly in the air...

"Really leaves you wide open, huh."

...I activated the intermediate fire sigil stone I'd readied...

The blast, vastly more intense in heat than its lesser counterpart's, flew vigorously toward Clammbon, which had smugly raised its pincers in the air.

The moment it collided with the crab, a terribly concussive sound shook the area. It felt a bit like an even stronger version of Nanami's Explosive Arrow. I bet she'd eventually reach this level of destruction with more leveling and training.

Now that I thought about it, the pace of Nanami's growth was the most abnormal out of all my party members'...

Orange flames engulfed the whole area, and an explosive gust brought the sweet smell of crabmeat along with it. I was hungry, so I would've loved to enjoy an early dinner, but unfortunately, this guy wasn't going down with a single stone.

There were still some leftover flames in the area, but I sprinted toward the crustacean regardless, its pincers still held aloft. I tried to slice it apart at the joints with my katana, but it thwarted me with its claws.

Immediately putting space between us, I sheathed my sword and prepared my sword-drawing arts. There, while using my Third and Fourth Hands to protect my flanks, I observed Clammbon's next moves.

The monster was a bit peeved. Its shell had turned red, and it was stamping its many feet, like a sewing machine set to max speed.

Guess the fiery shower was to blame for the red dye job.

While stamping its feet, Clammbon pointed its pincers at me and vigorously waved them up and down. A moment later, it sprayed a massive amount of bubbles in my direction before disappearing.

"Huh?"

Warding off the bubble-like projectiles, I found Clammbon again.

It was so ridiculously fast that I couldn't help but chuckle. It was almost like a colossal-size ghost crab. But the pincer it was sending my way was absolutely no laughing matter.

Even as I parried it with my Fourth Hand, the force of the collision threatened to knock me back. Unable to dampen the momentum, I was only able to prevent myself from being sent flying by bracing myself with my Third Hand.

Its assault didn't stop there. The next moment, it attempted to trample me, legs moving as fast as the needle of a sewing machine.

Protecting myself with my Fourth Hand, I moved out of the way. Clammbon then passed through where I had just been standing and made an arcing turn to stand in front of me. Then it trained its pincer on me, waving it up and down in the air.

I readied my Third and Fourth Hands and placed my real hands on my katana.

After it shook its claw up and down for a fourth, then fifth time, Clammbon suddenly made its move.

It opened its pincer and punched. One look told me that getting caught in that would be bad news, so I promptly jumped to the side.

Clammbon rushed past my previous position, came to a standstill a few paces later, and immediately raised its claws aloft.

Now was my chance. I ran straight toward the monster and used a fire sigil stone. It exploded, drowning the crab in flames, but I jumped straight into the blaze, throwing caution to the wind.

It was hot enough to sear my skin. Well, it probably *was* searing my skin. But I ignored that for the time being. I needed to tear off the boss's legs while it was stunned.

It was so hot I could scarcely open my eyes; I could hardly see a thing. But then, Mind's Eye must have kicked into gear. The more I focused, the clearer I could make out Clammbon's body. And its movements seemed way slower than they were before.

I drew my katana and aimed at its joints.

After I tore off several legs, it didn't take long. Going after each of the remaining off-balance crab limbs, one by one, was easy work. The boss occasionally swung its pincers down at me, but having lost several legs, it wasn't able to brace itself as it attacked. I didn't even have to block all of these blows, so in the end, the creature only left itself more exposed.

I sipped a healing potion and let out a sigh.

"This would've been a tough fight without these intermediate sigil stones...... Makes me a bit worried about the next leg of my journey."

I had a bumpy road ahead. From here, there was an abrupt spike in monster strength throughout the next group of floors.

"From thirty-one to forty, from fifty-one to sixty, and then from sixty-five onward, the monsters all get a lot tougher."

Still, that spike in power didn't mean they were unbeatable. I had come up with plenty of strategies to deal with them, too, so I knew I was going to be fine.

All right. It was time to break out the most basic, yet essential, skill required for all RTA speedruns.

"Now then, I've gotta pray like hell that no monsters show up, and run like my life depends on it!"

The first thing I thought when I arrived at the thirty-first layer was, *What the heck happened to the cave and ruins scenery I'd seen up until now?* The same thing had happened to me before, so it really wasn't that big of a surprise.

"Warm sunlight, a comfortable breeze, clear skies, and a sparkling stream. Just what is this place?"

I didn't even need to ask. This was a dungeon. Not somewhere to spread out a picnic blanket and enjoy sandwiches with everyone under the shade of the trees...... Sandwiches? I felt something in me shudder at the word, but that was probably my imagination.

Of the new monsters that started appearing on the thirty-first layer, the most troublesome would be...

"Pretty much all of them, I'd say!"

Birds, horses, sheep, snakes—no matter what type showed up, they were going to be extremely annoying to deal with.

I did think that I had gotten just about strong enough to clear layers thirty-one through forty. However, that was under the assumption that I was going through them together with a party.

I doubted I would lose in a one-on-one fight with any of these creatures, at least.

But if there were more enemies than that? Or if I had to fight one right after another? If I didn't have any healing items? The tables would undoubtedly turn against me.

If either Ludie or Nanami were with me, I would be able to get through approximately 80 percent of these encounters without using very many consumables. With both of them, we'd have been able to charge through it all without a care.

But for this excursion, I would have to dash through on my own.

You couldn't join the Three Committees without good grades, no exceptions. The question remained as to whether or not I could get good grades on the written exam. Maybe if I threw every ounce of effort I had toward studying, I could pull of a miracle and manage a good score.

However, the tests also have a practical component.

In the game, the exams are condensed, and you receive a score based on your stats. Because of that, I didn't know much about how they actually worked. Nevertheless, given that I'd been skipping not only my afternoon classes but my morning ones as well, not one ounce of me believed I could manage to pull off a good score. I was terrible with long-ranged attacks, for starters.

Still, the longer it took for me to bring my grades up, the more likely it was that I'd lose my chance to join the Three Committees entirely.

No matter what route you choose in the game, Takioto never joins the Three Committees to begin with. Another character would join them instead.

And since the Three Committees have a member cap, I wanted to join them as quickly as possible. I needed to get one step ahead of Iori.

Once I joined…then I supposed I'd make progress on the library event for the time being? No, I needed to be focusing on how to deal with the monster in front of me right now.

To compare its form to that of an anime, the monster was like a fusion of horse and human. With the lower body of a horse and an upper torso of a human, they were just as much of a standby in fantasy games as goblins—centaurs.

The instant I first saw a centaur in *Magical★Explorer*, I was absolutely blown away, for multiple reasons. I couldn't believe how they looked.

The horse half, I got. The splendidly toned and muscled lower body kicked hard against the earth and looked ready to rush off at a speed far beyond anything a human could match.

I could understand their weapons, too. A bow fit their design like a glove.

But why then, I wondered, did the human upper half look like a dapper, middle-aged man?

Eroge RPGs were typically happy to gender-swap centaurs into female versions. They were often designed with a busty and voluptuous upper body to complement their stout, equine lower bodies.

But the centaurs of *MX* are different. They are, without exception, handsome older men. When I'd first stumbled upon them while playing, it had been enough to make me question if this was really *Magical★Explorer* or not.

I'd seriously wondered at the time if I had been duped into buying a fake version of the game. It made me so suspicious that I messaged my friend about it and went on the game's message boards to double-check. Unfortunately, at the time, all this told me was that I was further along in the game than most.

Well, female centaurs appeared under a different name a few dozen layers down the line, and the feeling of relief I got from seeing them was still fresh in my mind. An eroge RPG without female centaurs in it was like strawberry milk without the strawberries.

Now, when it came to centaurs...

"It's their speed more than their weapon. That's the problem, really..."

The centaur readied its bow, conjuring a black arrow with magic and notching it in place. Then, it fixed its aim at me...and fired.

"Hngh!"

Exactly as it released its arrow, I opened up my Third Hand. It was faster than Nanami. I was able to easily repel the arrow, but the centaur readied its next arrow and immediately fired again.

While I dodged the attack, I decided to start running, both as a test and to take stock of the monster. Fortunately, this lone centaur was the only monster to appear.

"......Yup, they sure are fast."

The centaur held the advantage in terms of sheer speed. And while I hadn't looked into it at all, I surmised that it had me beat in stamina as well.

From there, though I tried to get away from the area as I warded off its attacks, I found myself in a bit of a sticky situation.

The monster was about as strong and fast as I'd expected. But what I hadn't anticipated was...

"I can't get away...!"

Using a last-ditch sound sigil stone to put a fair bit of distance between us, I was finally able to escape.

In the game, it was so easy to flee from enemies, too. Why exactly was it so hard in real life?

After mulling over why this would be the case, it finally hit me.

"Maybe it's got something to do with the environment?"

Up until now, I'd been mostly running away from enemies in interior locales; maybe that was why I'd been able to escape.

Before this layer, monsters that threatened me wouldn't often pursue me if I went down to the next layer. There had been a few exceptions, but in those cases, I'd just keep forging ahead, clearing floor after floor. Before I knew it, they would've stopped following me.

"What a fantastic view."

This area had so few places to hide that if you tried to play hide-and-seek here, the game would be over before it started.

I had a terrible feeling about this.

"Maybe there's some sort of requirement I've got to meet."

Perhaps I was in their territory, and they would keep chasing me until I left it. It seemed plausible.

For now, I set that aside as a potential explanation.

As for one other possible cause, maybe it was because I was weak?

But in *Magical ★ Explorer*, agility influenced your ability to escape. Sure, the centaurs were fast, but not so fast that I wouldn't be able to get away from them.

So what did it mean if I couldn't flee them?

For starters, it could indicate that I was wrong to assume things were the same as in-game. The game simply calculated things based on the numerical values of your character's speed and your opponents'. Your ability to escape ultimately depended on its results.

But here, I was up against real creatures. Living beings known as monsters. Maybe their decision to pursue me or not was a product of their instincts.

If that was the case, then this was really just nature taking its course.

"Maaaan, I really want to test some of this out............!"

I didn't have the time for that, though. Actual tests were one thing, but who knew how long it would take to gather data from a bunch of different angles and scrutinize the results.

What I could say for sure was that I needed to move fast. Staying here was only going to pointlessly waste time. Now that even running away had become its own ordeal, I needed to advance to the next layer, and the one after that, as fast as I could.

I glanced around the area. A vast grassland stretched out before me. In the distance, I got a brief glimpse of what seemed to be a monster.

"Truth is, my situation's not looking too great, huh?"

Escaping monsters wasn't my only problem.

"I have no idea if I should just keep on moving ahead or not."

When the dungeon had consisted of corridors alone, I could rely on the cardinal directions to know where I was going and to progress through them. With a flat, expansive floor like this, though, the two-dimensional game map and the three-dimensional world in front of me didn't match up as clearly.

If only I could make out some sort of landmark.

"If the spatial gate to the next layer was the same as the one I just went through, maybe that'll stand out?"

I remembered that when I arrived on this floor, there had been stone-work under my feet.

There was a magic circle on top of it as well, so maybe I just needed to search for some stone flooring to get to the next layer?

But just where would that be?

This didn't bode well for the rest of my expedition, considering this was still the very first layer after thirty.

For the time being, I had to hope. Hope that I'd find it soon.

"This is way too hard……"

After passing through the thirty-first layer and all the way to the thirty-third, something had started to dawn on me.

"If I see an enemy, I can't get too close."

Carelessly approaching them would start combat. Conversely, if I kept my distance, they would usually steer clear of me.

The catch, however, was that there were *a lot* of them.

"Yeeep, this is absolute murder…"

One-on-one fights, I was fine with. Although they'd take up a fair bit of time, I could win. But things got really tough when monsters showed up in the multiples, regardless of how much harder my sparring matches with Claris and the others may have been in comparison.

I'd been able to keep my spirits up for now, but if things got any more trying, I wasn't sure what was going to happen.

The fact that this was taking more time than anticipated was also weighing on me. I may have been bathed in warm sunlight, but this was a dungeon. Checking my watch, it was fair to say evening had set in, with dinnertime being only a few hours away. I had planned to be on the thirty-fifth layer by now.

For today, it would behoove me to rest after I finished taking down layer thirty-three. I was behind schedule, but I had accounted for needing one extra day anyway when I originally planned everything out, so I was still safe. If I needed to use this extra day of leeway, I had figured this would be where I'd end up using it, too.

This wasn't the only thing nagging at the back of my mind. I was also resorting to items more than I had anticipated. I'd intentionally bought extra so that I would have plenty to spare. But when I thought of how much dungeon I still had left to clear, I could foresee that extra buffer

running out. In the worst-case scenario, my supply might not last until the fortieth layer.

But there were some instances where I couldn't get away without expending items, leaving me no other options. Heck, I'd even had a few close calls after using them.

And in light of the monsters that appeared from the thirty-third layer on, I could tell my item consumption was going to accelerate.

Before me was a voluptuous female monster, loudly flapping her winged arms, which were nearly as big as I was, and staring down at me—a harpyia.

Harpyias were the monster I least wanted to encounter from layers thirty-one to forty. This partially came down to the same reason I'd been wary of the imps.

The imps were small and cute, while the harpyia were large and cute. Their facial features looked somewhat childish as well, so they resembled a well-developed adult with a youthful, girlish face.

If a harpyia walked into a bar, she was more likely than not to get ID'd at the door. Imps and knockers, meanwhile, were clearly *never* getting into the place to begin with.

There were several different things to pay attention to when fighting the harpyias. First was the swaying of their busty chests, freed from the vile scourge of clothing, along with the chestnut-colored bra holding them...... No, those weren't important, but, well, they did warrant *some* consideration......

What I really needed to look out for were the sharp, hawkish talons that extended out from their feet.

According to my research and what Yukine had told me, they'd aim those claws at me before swooping down on me from above. They would occasionally use wind magic, too.

The best measure for dealing with harpyias...?

"Running away from them, of course......"

But there was still a problem. Magic stones. While sound sigil stones and fire sigil stones were effective against them, they could be found on layers thirty-three through forty. That was a long stretch.

Was it wise for me to consume a magic stone every time one of them showed up?

My item usage had already gone through the roof fending off the horses and snakes, so could I really afford to use them on individual monster encounters? Considering the abilities they possessed, though, it seemed inevitable that I would have to resort to the items, even for one-on-one fights.

Though with this encounter now, I planned on using some stones to test if they would truly prove effective. Single monster encounters were the best for experimenting. I, for one, didn't know what would happen, so it was important to first secure the safest testing environment possible.

Taking a lesser sigil stone, I aimed it at the harpyia and activated it.

First was fire. Likely because I had seen the effects of the intermediate version, the fireball this stone produced looked piddly and unreliable. But the harpyia didn't want to get hit with it all the same, so she hastily dodged the attack.

She was fast.

This creature was probably the most agile out of all the monsters I had faced up until now. After evading, she immediately pointed her sharp claws at me and swooped down.

Slicing through the wind, she plummeted toward me, like a monster-sized arrow.

The monster was approaching with terrifying speed, but her attack was far too straightforward. Though it didn't look difficult to dodge, I decided to take the attack on purpose.

I stopped her with my Fourth Hand, using my Third Hand to prop myself up. There was a loud clang of metal meeting metal, and the impact rattled my whole body. However, it ended at that.

Compared to Clammbon, the creature's attacks were weak. They still proved annoying in other ways, though.

"Yeah, these chicks are seriously fast."

Using my Fourth Hand as a kickoff point, the harpyia flew back up into the air. This time, she opened her mouth wide and let out a loud shriek.

I couldn't help clicking my tongue. There were still a number of things I still wanted to test, but I probably needed to get away from here as soon as possible—or rather, it appeared that I was already too late.

Deflecting an arrow that flew in from my flank, I shifted my focus toward the attacker. Standing there was a centaur.

The most annoying thing with harpyias was that they would call for other monsters to come help. That would've been hugely beneficial if I were here to farm magic particles with an entire party. But going it alone, I was practically useless against flying monsters.

An arrow struck the ground at my feet with a *thud*. It must have been conjured with magic, for the next instant, it disappeared as if it had never been there at all, leaving behind only a hole in the dirt.

The centaur had come close to hitting me with those two arrows. But if I turned my attention to it, the harpyia was bound to swoop down and attack me, too.

Either that, or she would call for even more reinforcements.

I was clearly at a combat disadvantage. But was escape even an option here?

If I was going to take them down, I needed to do something about the harpyia first. Seeing as she was leisurely hovering in the air, I would have to resort to either primitive rock-throwing attacks or using consumable items.

In other words, escape was my *only* option here.

However, it took me another thirty minutes to fully escape from her.

"Harpyias are way too difficult to deal with."

Finishing my dinner, I was lost in thought as I sipped the coffee I'd brewed.

I had originally planned to be done with the thirty-fifth layer by now. In reality? I was currently on the thirty-fourth layer, and even though I hadn't taken a single step past the entrance, I was already about to turn in for the night.

I would be in trouble if things kept up like this. I needed a way of dealing with the harpyias, and I needed it now.

I understood a few things about them now, such as their extreme wariness. I also knew it would be difficult for me to get them out of the sky. I could manage dealing with just one of them, somehow. But they still had a trick up their sleeve that was tripping me up.

"There's gotta be something I can do about them calling for help......"

In the game, harpyias are useful eye candy that call more sources of experience points to you without you having to lift a finger. But that may have been why they were an absolute nuisance to escape from in real life.

It was also annoying that they didn't summon another one of their own, but a mobile centaur instead. Fortunately, the centaurs stopped showing up on the thirty-seventh layer, but that was still far off. Another annoying monster would show up later on, anyway, so it was a wash. If anything, the layers where those other monsters showed up more frequently would be even harder to deal with.

I'd known that this challenge was going to be difficult. But I'd assumed everything would work out if I just ran away; this was proving a lot more harrowing than expected.

Up until the thirtieth layers, it had been smooth sailing.

Nonetheless, it would've been difficult to anticipate this and try to get here even faster. There was nothing more I could've done to speed up my route, besides cutting down on breaks to keep sprinting past everything. Even if I'd skimped on resting as much as possible, however, that would have saved me a few hours at most. Would that have been worth it? Either way, I'd be pushing myself to my limits for sure.

The best solution to tackle the problem was likely the sound sigil stones. They had an effect on the evasive harpyias even without a direct hit, and I could create an opening the moment I activated it.

Unfortunately, however...

"I only have a few left......"

If it were possible to exchange my other magic stones for them, I would've done so in a heartbeat.

I had a little extra of each elemental magic stone besides fire. Should I have held off on buying them and opted for more sound sigil stones instead?

Nah, that would've been impossible. I couldn't have prepared the perfectly optimal item line-up without an initial test run. If anything, I should have been praising myself for preparing so well, all things considered.

Since sound sigil stones were comparatively inexpensive, maybe I had just used them too extravagantly?

At any rate, for now I needed to sleep. Staying up any later would affect my performance tomorrow.

My thoughts after overcoming the thirty-fourth and thirty-fifth layers were that they had gone much better, comparatively speaking.

Though I'd been in for a difficult battle whenever a harpyia showed up, by fleeing the moment I saw them and forging ahead, things had basically worked out.

Now that I was on the thirty-sixth floor, however, I would have to deal with yet another pesky opponent, albeit one not quite as tricky as the harpyias.

As it happened, the very first monster I encountered on this layer was a harpyia. Leaning up against a tree and basking in the sun, I just barely suppressed the urge to sneak up behind her and beat her to a bloody pulp. Instead, I put some space between us and ran off.

Though punching her to a pulp would've been a great way to blow off some steam, if another harpyia had noticed me and called for their friends, it would've been an absolute disaster.

After I progressed a bit, the thirty-sixth layer produced a new monster for me to stumble upon: the taotie.

The majority of a taotie's body resembles a sheep, but its face is like a guardian dog or lion statue, with sharp white fangs sprouting out from its mouth. If it bit me with those chompers, I bet it'd take a big chunk, or even worse, snap me clean in two. The curled horns sprouting from their heads made them resemble a fusion of a sheep and a guardian lion.

Though taotie had a few annoying attributes, the most bothersome was their speed. In *Magical★Explorer*, their agility stat is on par with that of centaurs. I was impressed, really, that they had the nerve to be so fast when their bodies were more sheep than anything else.

Unfortunately, it looked like running away from it would take me some time.

The taotie noticed my presence and stepped sideways with a loud growl to threaten me. When I filled my Third Hand with mana and approached it, the taotie spat fire in my direction.

In addition to their speed, their ability to attack from far away is also a nuisance.

Using my Third Hand to protect myself, I hastily moved from my position. The taotie followed my movements, changing the direction of its flames.

While the taotie's fire breath was more powerful than a lesser sigil stone, it was nowhere near the level of an intermediate one, so it wasn't too threatening. That being said…

"If they show up with centaurs and harpyias, I'm going to be in real trouble."

If monsters like centaurs and harpyias joined up with these things, which could pull off both melee-ranged attacks and spit fire from afar, I'd be dodging attacks from all angles.

With that in mind, I needed to break through this floor and the next quickly.

That's why I was calling it now. These areas, where it was one troublesome monster after another, would be where I'd expend most of my sigil stones.

Enchanting my Third Hand with water, I pushed forward through the taotie's flames. When the creature cut off its breath and pounced forward in an attempt to maul me, I sent it flying with my Fourth Hand. Then I used my sword-drawing arts.

A single taotie was worth taking on. So was a single centaur. Two or more, and I'd have to take stock of the area and decide whether to fight or flee. If there was a harpyia, I'd book it, even if it cost me a mountain of items in the process.

This sort of game plan ran through my head as I absorbed the taotie's magic particles and collected its magic stone.

Then, dashing off, I quickly ran into another encounter. Oh boy, I'd found it all right. Regretfully, it seemed my next opponent was a harpyia.

"Man, they might not have been total pushovers in the game, but you could still run away from them just fine."

To make matters worse, the harpyia was flanked by not one, but two taoties.

Were they out for a stroll? She'd picked a real nightmare crew to take on a walk. If the two taoties happened to be a couple, their kids would definitely make their little walks a lot more hectic.

While these boneheaded thoughts drifted through my head, I veered off the path. Unfortunately for me, there was a centaur on this side instead.

The harpyia's group was now closing in on me; guess I shouldn't have hesitated about how to proceed.

It would have been one thing if the taoties had stayed together, but as if to spite me, they'd cleanly split into two groups. It looked like they knew damn well how to corner their prey.

I promptly grabbed a sound sigil stone and prepared to activate it. I needed to decide before the centaur came over whether I was going to run away or clean this group up.

I aimed at the harpyia descending toward me and activated a fire sigil stone and sound sigil stone.

"……"

I couldn't get any words out.

I hadn't expected the thirty-sixth layer to be this trying. The special-made, high-quality uniform that Marino had excitedly ordered for me was in tatters.

While my body was unharmed, that was only thanks to my healing items. My mental state, on the other hand, was just as shredded as my clothing.

"What am I going to do……?"

At this point, moving was a hopeless endeavor. I needed to, yet I didn't want to move an inch. Even though I understood I was in serious trouble, I still didn't want to move.

Although I had somehow managed to get through the thirty-sixth layer, the remaining thirty-seventh, thirty-eighth, thirty-ninth, and fortieth meant I was still a long way from done. In spite of this, my body—or, more accurately, my mind—was totally spent. Night was fast approaching, so it was about time to have dinner and go to sleep.

But after waking up, I would need to conquer the remaining four layers and the boss in just one day.

Could I kick my pace into high gear starting tomorrow? Maybe if I had an unlimited supply of magic sigil stones. But in all honesty, that seemed impossible.

I'd ended up going through a serious amount of sigil stones on the thirty-sixth layer, and there was a distinct chance that I'd use up all the items I'd prepared before the fortieth layer. However, I needed to throw away the optimistic notion that I could preserve some of my magic stone stock on the thirty-seventh layer. The harpyia and taotie combo, plus the centaurs that backed them up, was dreadful.

My only saving graces were that the centaurs stopped appearing after the thirty-sixth layer, and monsters who moved even slower than the turtles in the Ancestral River Pool appeared instead.

Gah, these were exactly the times when I wanted to fix something up and have myself a delicious meal, even if it was simple.

But I wasn't in the mood to do anything.

Sheesh, this was an *awful* sign.

I picked out a few thick, filling cookies, unwrapped them, and tossed them into my mouth.

There were no two ways about it—things weren't looking good. My spirit was worn down, and I felt like I was losing the ability to feel anything.

Normally, I'd try to sing some songs from eroge to lift my spirits and help me refocus, but I couldn't get past a single verse before I gave up, exhausted. I couldn't even spare the energy to sing.

I understood that keeping my frame of mind steady was the most important thing of all, but I simply couldn't improve my mood.

I now had just three layers to go, but still, that was three whole floors. Would I really be able to reach the fortieth level in a single day?

The fortieth layer was home to a boss. Was I really in a state to take it on? I stared at the cookies I was forcing down.

They were chalky and dry. Tasted awful. Even when I chased them with coffee, I didn't feel satisfied at all.

A bath. I really wanted to take a bath. Rinse off in a hot shower, use the luxurious tub in Marino's house, and stretch out my arms and legs nice and slow.

What if I just went back up to the surface from here?
The thought crossed my mind.

I had gotten plenty far enough, hadn't I? If I went back now, I was guaranteed to get the top score in the class, and I'd be able to join the Three Committees, too. I might not be able to claim the first-time clear bonus, but there were still other places I could grab the same item at some point. This was just the fastest way to get it, and with the easiest conditions to meet.

The more and more I thought about it, the more I felt fine with it. That nothing was more dangerous than pushing yourself too far.

I could challenge this dungeon whenever I wanted. I couldn't afford to die.

When I shoved my hand in my pocket, I felt three square objects beside my return stone.

I took them from my pocket.

They were protective charms.

One had unbelievably clean stitching, so beautiful it was as if a machine had sewed it all. Embroidered on its surface were a small waterfall and the stream it fed into.

The second was composed of high-quality white fabric and featured an image of a maid wearing an extra-long scarf.

The seams of the final protective charm were, honestly, not very good. However, they were securely stitched and kept everything from coming apart, and there was a clover embroidered in the bottom right corner.

All of a sudden, I thought back to an event in the Hanamura house.

I'd returned from turtle-farming with Nanami to find Yukine, Ludie, and Claris cleaning up the living room in a mad rush. They seemed a bit standoffish, too, as if they were trying to keep what they were doing a secret.

Noticing them, Nanami appeared slightly displeased as she elbowed me gently and said, "You lucky dog, you." When I heard her mumble, "If I just had the time…no, I'll just push myself to fit it in somewhere…" I told her off.

"So take a damn break, then. You work way too much."

"Do you wish to rob me of my moment of supreme bliss, Master?!"

"How the hell is the time you spend working a 'moment of bliss'?!"

From there, we devolved into our normal comedy routine, with Claris being the first one to see us and chuckle. Marino, who had come home at some point, prepared tea and coffee for us. Sis merely listened along in silence, though she appeared to be enjoying our display. And before I knew it, Yukine and Ludie joined in, and we were all laughing away.

The following day, Yukine had handed me a protective charm with a shy smile. Told me she was "praying for my success."

After that, Nanami had gifted me a charm, too. She had seemed slightly out of it a few days before that, so she must've been pulling all-nighters to finish it. Ludie had looked so worried, I'd thought she would cry.

Then... Her arms wrapped around my body, my hands over hers.

I gripped the charms in my hand tightly.

I thought that I'd try going just a bit longer.

I wasn't going to give up.

Now that I was blowing through my items left and right, I was able to easily get through the thirty-seventh layer—so easily that it was like the thirty-sixth had never even happened.

Well, actually, I must've had a really rough go of it. The amount of time it had taken made that clear.

Still, I was in this strange sort of trance where the hardships didn't feel so hard. My thoughts were also perfectly clear, for a reason I couldn't quite pin down.

After getting through the thirty-seventh floor, layers thirty-eight and on were a breeze. The harpyia appearance rate dropped drastically, replaced by a kind of slow-moving bull monster. The things were so sluggish, they were practically begging me to run away from them.

Another advantageous change was that when the harpyias did show up, they now called bulls to their aid.

What did they expect to get out of calling those slowpokes? I simply used the opening to deal with the harpyia and left the summoned bulls in the dust.

Continuing on like this, I reached the fortieth layer around noon. I was overjoyed that I had gotten used to these levels, along with the harpyia. That, and I was glad that more low-agility monsters had stared to show up. I got through almost all the floor without getting bogged down in difficult fights.

However, my stock of sound sigil stones was empty.

Even if I still had some, though, the time to use them had passed.

I took a leisurely lunch in front of the magic circle that led to the fortieth-layer boss. For some reason, my magic stone stove wasn't working properly, so I used a lesser fire sigil stone to send some fallen branches and leaves up in flames.

Thanks to that, I was able to heat up some soup and brew some hot coffee.

Up until now, I hadn't ever once lit a fire with a sigil stone. I panicked when the force of the flames originally scattered the branches and tinder I had gathered together. I couldn't help smiling when I looked down at the miserable sight left behind after everything had blown apart.

I was in a fantastic mood. Now, there was just one floor left.

What did I do after finishing lunch? I lay down and took a break. I wanted to challenge the boss in tip-top shape.

Because appearing on the fortieth layer wouldn't be the original boss that regular students faced when they came this far, but a hidden boss that only appeared during a solo first-time clear.

There was an arena, the kind that looked like it would be at home in some European ruins. An oval field where gladiators clashed, encircled by seats for an audience.

But there was no one seated in the stonework galleries, and I was the only soul standing in the arena.

Then, a single ray of light shone on the opposite side of the arena from where I was. Looking toward the source of the light, I could make out a single silhouette.

I gently touched the charms I had fastened to my bag, like I was patting a child on the head, before taking a deep, deep breath. Then, I placed them in my pocket.

Slowly, a man descended from the sky. On his back sprouted two gray wings, and without flapping them once, he touched down on the ground.

He wore armor that resembled that of the ancient Romans, with a sword nearly three feet in length secured to the strap at his waist. On his arm was fastened a circular metal shield.

He turned to me, folding up the wings at his back. They were like the wings of an enormous swan.

His appearance bore a close resemblance to images of angels found in paintings.

I knew different, though. He was no angel.

"Hello, Icarus."

Naturally, of course, he didn't say a word back. His handsomely chiseled face didn't move a muscle, and he continued to stare hard at me. I placed my hand on my sword and reinforced the mana flowing through my stole. Only when I took a step toward him did he finally draw his sword.

Swinging my body in a side-to-side feint, I sent a punch from my Third Hand toward Icarus.

I thought I had put a fair amount of force in my punch, but Icarus hunkered down and took the full impact with his shield. He didn't budge an inch from where he stood.

I sent my Fourth Hand out in front of me to take his blade, swinging toward me as if in payback for my previous attack. I thought that I would then use the opening to release my sheathed sword. However...

"Just how much muscle does this dude have? Nearly sent me flying......"

I needed to be more careful about blocking his attacks. The weight behind each was even greater than Clammbon's. Quickly discarding any thoughts of going on the offensive, I focused myself on dodging. Icarus's follow-up attacks came at me in rapid succession. Sometimes it was his sword, sometimes his shield, and sometimes his legs.

He was also faster than the harpyias. All his stats were head and shoulders above the monsters I had seen up to now.

But that was to be expected. Icarus wasn't a boss that was supposed to show up on the fortieth layer. He was a deep-layer class of monster, placed here to challenge beefed-up characters going through their second playthrough.

If a party who struggled to get through the fiftieth layer tried to take him on, they'd definitely lose. Even I would be almost guaranteed to bite the dust if I hadn't prepared. And my victory was still far from guaranteed. He was simply that strong.

Icarus slowly floated up and flew into the air, then pointed the tip of his sword toward me. Rays of sunlight reflected off the blade.

The moment only lasted long enough for me to think: *I've got a bad feeling about this.*

Sword still pointing straight at me, Icarus began his descent. He rapidly began picking up speed.

All of a sudden, I remembered that the stoop of a peregrine falcon was faster than a bullet train. At that instant, a cold chill went down my spine.

My entire body was telling me I couldn't afford to take this hit. Channeling all the strength I could muster into my legs, feet, and limbs (Third and Fourth Hand included), I immediately dashed away, evading the blow.

A burst of air.

Whoosh... No, it wasn't a simple sound like that. It was like the loud *GWOOOO* of a rocket. A direct hit would send me flying at best and tear me to pieces at worst. One wrong step and I'd meet my doom.

However, I had fully prepared a way to counter it.

"Do you know how many stupid knockers I had to fight to get all of these?"

Icarus flew back up in the air again, and I put all of my strength into dodging his swoop attack. He seemed to realize his attack wasn't working, so he flew in low toward me.

I purposefully blocked the full blow of Icarus's sideways sweep as he closed in. Then, using the momentum of his attack to jump sideways, I activated a sigil fire stone (intermediate) and aimed it at his wings.

"_____!"

Icarus's weakness was fire. The game developers must've taken a page out of the original Greek myth. The story of Icarus flying high with his wax wings, only to melt as he drew close to the sun, was known far and wide.

Seriously, thank goodness he had this weak point to exploit. Without it, my solo run through the first forty layers would have been doomed from the start.

His wings melted, and he roared a silent scream as he fell to the ground. Then he cast a sharp glare toward me, so I consoled him with another attack.

Just as I got ready to make my follow-up strike, however, he rolled away and retreated backward.

Icarus was now a shadow of his once angelic-looking self.

His splendid wings had melted away; there were now two white, sinewy muscles stretching from his back where his wings had once been. With his body also burned dark red by the flames, he looked terribly pathetic.

He wasn't discouraged, though. Standing up, he pointed his sword my way and fixed his eyes on me.

Right after he kicked off the ground with his legs, he swung his sword at me. Whether it was from losing his wings, or from his burns, I couldn't tell, but the power of his swing had dulled slightly. But right after confirming his strike wouldn't go through, he changed his approach, occasionally using his shield to push me and create some sort of opening as he assaulted me from all angles.

As I watched him boldly rise in the face of his injuries, a thought suddenly crossed my mind:

What strength he has.

Icarus really was incredible. His wings were gone, his body was burned, so he could've easily felt totally defeated. Yet he'd gotten back up despite it all. Not only that, but he was pressuring me with attacks that were even more innovative than before.

Watching him, I thought:

This is the type of guy I wanna be like.

What exactly was my strength? Where did it come from?

Kousuke Takioto's vast mana pool? Power derived from my knowledge of the game? Might earned through my effort and training?

All of that was probably part of it.

But was that really all there was to it? Could I have gotten to this layer with that alone?

I could definitely say it would've been impossible.

I probably would've been bested along the way. I would've gotten discouraged. Clammbon might have even proven too much for me. I might've ended up encircled by harpyias and killed.

It was thanks to my friends that I'd been able to battle my way here. No doubt about it.

If Claris hadn't coached me nearly every day, if Yukine hadn't empathetically taught me sword techniques, if Ludie hadn't helped me out with my special training regime, if Sis and Marino hadn't shared their knowledge of locations, tools, and more, I surely would've stumbled somewhere along the way.

It was a strange sensation. For reasons unknown, even as my thoughts drifted beyond the battle in front of me, I was still able to parry or dodge every single one of Icarus's attacks.

The more I concentrated, the more his movements seemed to slow......

How many times had our blades clashed by now?

Icarus must've thought he was getting nowhere. He was stepping in closer to me, slashing sideways with his weapon faster and more wildly than before. Still, I had a clear grasp of his swordplay. I took an attack with my Third Hand and pretended to lose my balance.

Icarus must've taken this to be his chance. Trying to press me further, he bashed his shield in my direction. But my Fourth Hand was there to defend me from it.

In that instant, it seemed to him that my guard was full of holes. He swung his sword high up into the air. The blade gleaned in the sunlight as it bore down. I drew my katana in sync with his timing.

I could win.

Unfortunately, things didn't go that way. My slice bounced off his body, barely leaving behind a scratch.

"_____"

What had happened? Right then, I was sure I had cleaved Icarus in two. But my sword hadn't gone through.

As I quickly opened up space between us, I looked the monster over, unconsciously muttering to myself.

"No way........"

Wave after wave of yellow magic was flooding out of Icarus's body.

What in the world was this phenomenon? Actually, no, I knew of a similar event. This was his rage mode.

In *Magical ★ Explorer*, rage mode triggers when a monster's HP falls below a set amount, powering up all its stats. That's what ended up activating right at that moment. However, the Icarus I was familiar with wasn't supposed to enter rage mode without his wings.

No, that wasn't what I needed to think about. I had to concoct a strategy, and fast. Though that was my intention, something even more unanticipated happened that left me even less room to breathe.

Icarus actually threw his shield aside and brandished swords in both of his hands.

Still shaken by the unexpected development, the boss kicked off the ground and jumped straight toward me, swinging both his swords down.

The attack was hefty.

Despite defending with my Third and Fourth Hands, the force of the blow nearly sent me tumbling. I sensed his speed and his strength had risen several levels.

My follow-up strike also made another thing abundantly clear: Icarus's body had become outlandishly tough.

Considering my sword had only left a surface scratch, it must have gotten substantially harder. Also, while his enraged mode movements still seemed slow to me, if I couldn't match his speed, it was ultimately meaningless. At that moment, I was just barely able to keep up.

I bet he'd tossed his shield aside because his defense had shot up so much that he wanted more attack power to compensate. Either that, or he was trying to get faster by shedding any weight he could.

Damn. This wasn't fair. Why'd his body have to harden like that? Had he given up his humanity? No, this was a dungeon. It was entirely plausible that he was actually some sort of non-human entity disguised as a person.

Icarus and I fell into a deadlock.

Since I was focused solely on defending myself, none of his hits were landing. However, it seemed like none of my blows were having an effect on him.

I launched my katana from its sheath. Icarus blocked it with his sword. I punched with my Third Hand. He recoiled from the punch briefly before bouncing back like nothing had happened.

Things were going downhill.

Suddenly, Icarus backed off, opening up a large amount of space between us.

He must have been preparing to use some kind of magic against me. I prepared for it by positioning my stole in front of me and glared back at him.

Icarus didn't launch any magic at me. But the mana around him sure was expanding.

Was he telling me he was going to finish me off here? I could tell that even more mana began rushing through his body.

I really didn't think I could win.

His basic appearance wasn't any different from before. But my Mind's Eye told me that this version of Icarus was practically another being compared to the one I had been fighting up until now.

I was barely hanging on already; would I really be able to absorb his attack? And was I really going to end up losing here? Was this how everything up until now was going to end?

I put my hand against my pocket.

When I did, I felt a slight bulge. Confirmation that my protective charms were inside.

All of a sudden, I remembered my training with Yukine and Claris. The two of them had patiently helped me practice. Afterward, they'd looked at me covered in sweat and jokingly remarked, "Would you like a towel? A bath? Or maybe me?" I wonder what would've happened if I had actually chosen the third option?

After I was done with my bath, Ludie gave me a massage out of the blue, with her awkward, uncustomed hands. She'd been raring to do it, too. Unfortunately, compared with Nanami and Yukine, she wasn't very skilled. And on top of that, she demanded I pay her back with a cup of instant ramen after I finished! But seeing her self-satisfied grin had energized me a bit.

Oh yeah, I was going to buy some instant ramen on my way home today. Then I'd get to see that smug smile of hers again.

Right, I needed to buy some and head home. In that case, I couldn't afford to give in now, could I?

What exactly was I supposed to do here? What was my counterplay?

Using sigil stones was one option. What if they didn't have an effect, though? My Sword-Drawing Arts—Flash—maybe? But it had only been able to cut through a thin layer of skin.

If Yukine was here, she'd be able to cut through. If she was here......
Yukine............?

Suddenly, her figure flitted through my mind. Her beautiful

swordplay appeared in the back of my head. I took that image and placed it over myself.

With that blade, with her skills...Yukine would've been able to cleave Icarus in two.

I turned my attention to the boss and drew in a deep breath.

I didn't know why, but right now, I felt like I could reproduce it. I couldn't perform a chain of attacks like Yukine. But if I used everything that I had in me, dedicated it all to a single slash, I got the sense I could copy it. I'd have to pour my whole body into this single release. But would replicating her techniques in a single attack be enough?

I superimposed my memory of Yukine, stuck fast like glue in my mind, over myself. What had she been like at the time? Calm and composed; loose and free of tension; then, with a single breath, straight out in front of her...

I slowly removed my hand from my uniform pocket.

What a mysterious thing. I felt as if I could move my body like she could. Then, from behind me I felt Ludie, Nanami, and Sis. Like everyone was at my back, supporting me.

Finished gathering his power, Icarus let out a wild roar as he kicked off from the ground.

His body gleamed with a pale golden light. With a seething, bestial look in his bloodshot eyes, he rushed at me like a hurricane. He held both swords behind him mere inches off the ground, ready to scrape against it at any moment.

I could tell he was sending mana into to his arms and his swords as he drew closer. He was coming at me with enormous, massive power behind his strike, beyond any other attack I had faced so far.

Strangely, I wasn't scared at all. Nor was I nervous. All I saw in front of me was that flashing blade.

I bent my knees and placed my hand on my katana. Building up mana in my sheath, I stared down Icarus looming in front of me.

Icarus brought his sword up in a slash. One beat behind him, the mana inside my sheath exploded, and the blade pressed in toward him.

A loud metallic *clang* echoed through the arena.

It had come from Icarus's arm and sword.

A look of astonishment came over his face. He must've seen my earlier technique and assumed I wouldn't be able to cut him. But this was no longer my usual Flash.

With everyone pushing me forward, and the glint of Yukine's blade-work in my eye, I could pull it off for the very first time... The next-level Flash.

I directed my last sigil fire stone (intermediate) at Icarus, who was still gripped by shock.

I didn't understand why, but I could see a faint line. Somehow, I knew that slicing through the line was my key to cleaving through Icarus. And in that case, all I needed to do was cut it.

I just had to face that line and send my gleaming strike down the middle.

Then, my body burning up inside, I once again sent my blade toward the moaning Icarus.

"Second Form—Flash—"

The instant he transformed into a magic stone the size of my fist, a gorgeously ornate treasure chest appeared in the middle of the arena.

When I opened it, I found tiny glowing seeds inside. Taking a few in my hands, I clenched them tightly.

I had finally gotten them. The items you needed to turn a sub-character into the mightiest of all.

Items that removed all limits on a character's growth—Seeds of Possibility.

When you swallow one of these in-game, all the upper limits to your abilities vanish, enabling you to freely level your stats up as high as you please. When you combine these in a new game with an item that lowers your level, you can build characters up to the peak of their potential. That isn't all, either. Certain characters, including Kousuke Takioto, also gain the ability to use a wide variety of weapons after you use a Seed of Possibility on them.

This item was completely unnecessary for Iori or the developers' favorite heroines. They could grow even stronger with them, of course. But Iori and those heroines could obtain a monstrous level of power without them.

For me, though, I couldn't do without them. Seeds of Possibility, as the name suggested, nourished any and all possibilities in a character. With this, the sky was the limit......

And from here on out, I wouldn't need to venture into dungeons by myself anymore.

"Wild. I don't know why, but... Suddenly, I feel like the Seeds of Possibility don't really matter at all."

True, I was happy to get my hands on them. After all, look at how much I'd gone through to do so.

I was definitely excited about it, sure.

What was it then? I had the feeling I had already received a power much greater than what the Seeds of Possibility could offer.

More than any joy I felt from obtaining the Seeds of Possibility, another far greater emotion filled me up inside. It then raged inside my heart.

I wanted to see them.

To get out of here as fast as I could and see them all. And to tell them.

They might all tell me I was absolutely crazy. Or be baffled that I would say something like this out of the blue.

But I still wanted to see them and let them know.

I put all the Seeds of Possibility away in my bag and used the spatial magic circle to head outside.

Outside of the dungeon, a blue sky, though not entirely free of clouds, stretched out above me. Despite being hit with the sun's rays, it wasn't especially hot, so I was plenty cool in my tattered uniform.

Watching the few clouds drift along in the blue, I took a deep breath.

There was a bit of an earthy smell in the air, and I deludedly thought that things had been better in the dungeon I just exited. Except the dungeon's clear skies occasionally had harpyias flying through them, so the blue above me was decidedly the better of the two.

Turning my eyes away from the sky above, I thought about whether I should immediately head home, or if it was better to send everyone a message first. But just as I headed off, someone greeted me from behind.

"I've been waiting for you, Master."

Standing there was Nanami.

Clad in her usual maid attire, she gracefully bowed before me.

"Huh, why're you here? I told you I wasn't sure when I'd end up getting back, right?" I said, prompting a chuckle from her.

"Once you're as experienced as I am, it's easy enough to predict when exactly you'll be coming home, Master," she boldly declared.

What the heck was she on about?

Nanami puffed up her chest, stretching her maid uniform to its seams, and gave a smug smile. When my eyes drifted past her, I noticed something.

I got a better look and saw a freestanding hammock with a wooden stand in the shade of a tree. Next to it was an expensive-looking circular table with a tea set and some sort of cookies placed on top with a pile of books.

Predict when I'd come home…? Yeah, right. She had been waiting here the whole damn time.

She smoothly shifted her body to try and hide the hammock and table. But that was never going to work, so naturally, I could easily still see everything.

"Honestly, who in the world would be drinking black tea in a place like that? They must be getting in the way."

She clicked her tongue and had an irritated tone to her voice, but obviously, it was her. Actually, wait, so she knew that was black tea, then?

As I mulled over the best way to shoot down her explanation, a voice suddenly came from behind me.

"You, are you a friend of hers?"

I turned to the source of the voice and found an older cleaning lady standing there.

"That girl. For the past two days, she's refused to move an inch no matter what I say to her. And she's been getting in my way the whole time. Tell her to hurry up and head home for me."

She heaved a sigh and left. I felt bad for the exhausted woman, but I couldn't help smiling. I could easily imagine Nanami using her twisted logic to quibble with the cleaning woman. Next time I saw her, I'd be sure to apologize.

With a nonchalant look, Nanami turned awkwardly in the other direction.

"Oh, look over there, a butterfly."

"I think it's safe to drop the act now."

"Putting that aside for now, Master!"

Changing the topic seemed to be her strategy of choice. Oh well, I didn't really care about pushing the point any further, so I let her ignore it.

"What?"

She quickly gave a very maid-like curtsey.

"Congratulations on besting forty layers."

Hearing this, it suddenly came to me. Now that she'd mentioned it, I hadn't checked yet. Despite having a simple way to definitively verify my feat. I'd beaten Icarus and gotten my hands on the seeds, so I figured that counted as clearing down to layer forty, but I still needed to make sure.

"Oh yeah, now that you mention it."

"...You did get through forty layers, didn't you?"

I couldn't help my wry smile at the suspicious look she gave me.

It felt a bit like that wasn't what was important right now, and I didn't really care about my forty-layer challenge anymore. I took out my student ID and checked what finished dungeon layers it had recorded for me.

On it, next to "Tsukuyomi Academy Dungeon" were the words "Fortieth Layer." The student ID automatically updated itself to show how much of the dungeon you'd conquered, but just what sort of mechanism allowed it to do this, anyway?

"Yup, I cleared all forty."

When I showed the proof to Nanami, her expression loosened, and like a flower, a bright smile bloomed across her face.

"Wonderfully done, Master. However, judging from your current state, you must be quite exhausted."

She had a point; my clothes were in tatters. However, my body itself was spotless. The power of healing items was nothing to sneeze at.

"With your permission, allow me to hug you close and pat you on the head. I assure you it shall relieve your fatigue."

With the same composed expression as usual, Nanami put out her arms. I bet she was joking. She had to be thinking I'd reply with my usual, "What the hell are you talking about...?" However, the current Kousuke wasn't going to do anything like it.

"Well then, if you insist."

I quickly placed my arms around her without hesitation. Then I gently stroked Nanami's head and wrapped myself around her. I buried my face in her beautiful silver hair and took a deep, long breath.

She was warm. Her hair was silky smooth. The smell of Nanami.

Warmth filled my body. It felt as though all the sludgy buildup inside of me was slowly being purged.

But more than anything else......I was unbelievably happy. Overjoyed to know she had been waiting in a place like this for two whole days.

"Uh, um, M-M-Master?"

At first, she fidgeted and tried to resist. Before long, however, she gave in and succumbed to my embrace. At last, she wrapped her arms around my body.

After I'd gotten my fill of Nanami, I slowly separated from her. She stared back vacantly, her face flushed red as if feverish.

"Thanks to you...all my exhaustion's been swept away."

It must've been because I'd hugged her so suddenly. Her hair was a bit disheveled. Nanami herself didn't seem like she planned to fix it, so I approached her and combed it back into place with my hands. I then gently patted her on the head. Staring at me with upturned eyes, Nanami seemed on the verge of saying something, but she ultimately stayed silent.

"Kousuke!"

As I patted her head, two women came running up to where we stood.

Yukine, clad in her uniform, with a naginata strapped to her back.

Then Ludie, casting aside any hint of ladylike grace as she ran over, despite her attempts to play the part of a noble princess at school.

A great big grin spread across both their faces as they made their way over.

I caught Ludie in my arms with a *thud* as she charged into me.

"Ludie, Yukine... What're you doing here?"

I hadn't even messaged anyone yet.

"We heard from Nanami. After that...... What's wrong, Nanami?"

Apparently, she'd gotten in touch with both of them before coming to greet me. She really was the best maid around.

Still wrapped in my arms, Ludie stared at Nanami and cocked her head. The maid did look different than usual; right now, she was several times cuter than normal. I suppose I was the one to blame for that, though.

"Nanami's fine, you don't need to worry about her. More importantly, aren't classes going on right now?"

It would have made sense for them to come yesterday, when

afternoon classes had been canceled due to morning exams. But that wasn't the case today. At this time of day, afternoon classes should still be going on... Though, they were set to end soon.

"Indeed, I skipped out to come here."

"Me too."

Hearing them tell me so clearly, I felt happiness well up inside me.

Honestly, what were they thinking? A hopeless pair, truly. Why'd they go that far for a guy like me...?

I needed them to put on the brakes. I felt so very, very giddy, there was no telling when it'd all come spilling out.

When I put a bit more force into my hug, Ludie answered by squeezing down with her own, too.

"...Sheesh, are you sure that's a good idea? Especially you, Yukine. You're supposed to be the vice president of the Morals Committee, aren't you?" I said, turning my sights to Yukine, who replied with a grin.

"That's a real good point, actually. I just wanted to tell off this troublemaker who decided to skip school during exam week to jump into a dungeon, see."

Ha ha. When she put it like that, there was nothing I could really say back.

"*Ha-ha-ha,* I'm sorry."

"It's fine, I picked a class that would be okay to slip out of even if news got around."

Yukine laughed. Then, catching her breath a moment, she broke into a big gentle smile.

"Besides, I was real worried, too..."

"......Sorry."

The next person to arrive was even more out of place than Yukine. As she walked over, I burst into laughter.

"Sis? What're you doing here?"

Classes were still going on, right? Why the heck was she here, then? Two students being here was already bad enough, but you're supposed to be a teacher, Sis. It's afternoon period now, right? Even if she didn't have any classes, she had exams to grade or plenty of other work to be doing, right?

"I heard you came back."

Her, too, huh? Dammit, all she'd done was come to see me, so why did I feel so giddy about it?

"You did, huh…,…? Well, all right. I'm back, Sis."

"Mm-hmm. Welcome back."

"I got through the fortieth layer."

"Yeah. I thought so."

"Aren't classes going on right now?"

"They are. I had my students switch to self-study."

Unbelievable. Seriously, what were you doing? How was I supposed to hold back my smile at an answer like that?

Heck, even worse than that, my freaking tear glands were at their limit here. I was getting too damn giddy. Seriously, why did everyone have to come and see me?

"Kousuke," Sis said, taking one step, and then another, toward me. Just when I thought she couldn't get any closer, she stretched out her arms and wrapped them around me.

"You did a good job."

"Yeah. I really gave it my all."

I wiped my tears from my eyes as Sis reluctantly stepped away from me.

I'd leave it up to Marino or Ms. Ruija to chide her about cutting class. There was something more important I needed to do.

"Hey, everyone, can I say something? Um, well, see, there's something I want to let you all know…"

I was going to need to pass on the same thing to everyone who would get here later.

"As you all know already, I was able to accomplish my goal of clearing the fortieth layer."

The latter half had been a lot more trying than I imagined. Still, I'd managed to get through it all somehow. And what was the secret to my success?

It was, without a doubt…

"It's thanks to all of you I was able to grow this strong."

Throughout my daily training, there had always been someone there with me.

Everyone's coaching and teaching dwelled in each one of my movements in combat.

Being alone with my back against the wall had convinced me.

Convinced me just how much support I had received from everyone.

"When I was close to giving in, everyone's faces would pop up in my mind. It gave me the strength to hang in there."

How many times had I thought about turning back?

How many times had I thought about giving up?

How many times had they saved me when I was in pinch?

Nanami, her face still slightly flushed. Ludie, listening with a solemn expression. Yukine, beaming, and Sis, looking the same as always. I gazed at each of them.

My mind suddenly went back to my resolution at the waterfall.

I wanted to take everyone to their happy endings. I wanted to get stronger with that in mind.

It was a one-sided sentiment. I had thought it would be something I'd single-handedly devote myself to achieving, no matter how banged up I got in the process.

But it hadn't been a one-sided sentiment. Everyone had given me so much thought, helped me out so much. The people I wanted to protect were there for me, the people I loved were there for me.

Honestly, I had to be the luckiest person in the whole dang world.

I wiped away my overflowing feelings with a tattered shirt sleeve. Then, I tightly gripped the three protective charms in my pocket.

All right then, it was time to let it all out. The gratitude threatening to burst out of my chest. These feelings of mine.

To convey it all to the irreplaceable people, far, far more precious to me than any paltry Seeds of Possibility.

"Thank you."

Exhaustion built up right under your nose. Even if you were feeling perfectly energized, an innocuous trigger could make it all come crashing down around you.

In my case, the trigger was a hot shower and a soft, comfy bed.

The fatigue from my fight with Icarus and everything I'd gone through beforehand. The mental stress worrying about whether I'd be able to conquer all forty layers.

Of course I would be dead tired.

I slipped into bed, not giving a second thought to the possibility that Sis might be hiding in there. I was so beat, I didn't want to move to another room. After snatching half the pillow away from her, I immediately shut my eyes.

The warmth and softness around me made me feel dreamy, but I figured it had to all be a pleasant dream. Both my blanket and the area beside me were warm for some reason, so I quickly fell asleep.

Everything up until then had been well and good. The problem was now.

The birds weren't chirping. The sun had risen high into the sky, and it was time for brunch, more than breakfast.

Truth was, I had planned on waking up earlier. I had intended to go to school like normal and hear Orange tell me, "What the hell're you skipping exams for, dude?!" while Iori glared at me in shock, sending shivers down my spine.

Apparently, Nanami had arbitrarily decided to let me sleep in. I hoped she was ready for me to tell her off for it.

Looking at a message from Ludie, I realized that she had been worried about how exhausted I was and had also let me be. Well, clearly there was no reason to get angry at such a thoughtful gesture as that, right?

After a slightly early lunch with Claris and Nanami, I sent a message to Ludie and the others that I was getting ready to head to school. Then I left the house, with Claris seeing me off at the door.

By the time I arrived at the Academy, grades would already be posted.

I wondered what was going to happen to my place at school. I sort of felt that since I hadn't been coming there lately, maybe everyone had forgotten about me. Though, they'd all remember really quick if they saw me walking with Ludie. That went double for those LLL guys.

No matter how this situation played out, they would still see me as their enemy. Though whether my exam results would harden or soften their hostility, I couldn't say. The only thing I could say for sure was that it didn't matter to me either way. However…

I glanced over at Nanami walking beside me.

If any harm extended to the people I cared about, then it was all-out war. Actually, I felt like Ludie would be the one to blow up at them first. Though, Nanami was cute enough to have a fan club of her own, so I didn't think it would ever come to that.

I was surprised to see Ludie standing in front of the school gate.

When she spotted me, she adjusted her posture and waved at me with ladylike modesty. Seeing her wave, Nanami said:

"I've always found it strange, but it's amazing she's managed to keep up that facade of hers."

I felt the exact same way.

Apparently, grades had popped up on the magical bulletin board just before lunchtime. Everyone had planned on going to see them after they were done eating, but Ludie had been the only one to see my message and come meet me.

She and I walked side by side, with Nanami following along behind us.

We couldn't help sticking out. The Imperial Princess Ludivine. The stunning maid beauty, Nanami. And a boy in a gaudy stole.

Today, however, the usual sharp glares of jealousy weren't coming my way. And people weren't looking on with envy, either.

No, they were staring with fear and dread, as though gazing at some strange, otherworldly being.

Everyone we walked past was looking at me. Normally, most people's eyes gravitated toward Ludie. The dirty looks they gave me were just a little bonus.

However, today was different. Absolutely everyone had their eyes on me.

Ludie seemed somehow happy as she glanced around.

Then, in a voice just loud enough for me to hear at her side, she said, "What a wonderful feeling." Even Nanami seemed to be in high spirits, though she looked the same as ever.

I began to think everyone was just going to stare at me like this, but that was not to be.

"Oh, hey, Kousuke!" Orange called out to me. "Y'know, I was about to be, like, 'Why do you get to skip out on exams?' but you were up to some serious stuff, man! You should've looped us in, too, dude!"

Orange wasn't the only one. The other boys and girls in my class all sang my praises. Then, talking to me like any other classmate, they ribbed me for skipping class too much or demanded I bring them into the dungeon as punishment for keeping them out of the loop, before they eventually went on their way.

I responded pretty awkwardly, I think. What was I supposed to do, though? I hadn't been expecting any classmates, except maybe Orange, to treat me like normal. A guy like me, with a mountain of bad gossip to his name.

Ludie explained things to me as I watched everyone depart, dumfounded.

"Actually, Hijiri went around and stuck up for you with all our classmates. You better be sure to thank him for it, later."

Honestly, I'd assumed only the people closely associated with the Hanamura house would look at me free of prejudices. But I was wrong.

"Really? Gotcha. I'll be sure to thank him."

I still had one question, though. Was Iori really all that friendly with the no-name girls in our class? He was generally a pretty late bloomer with women. Though, when it came to the heroines, in some ways he was a really *early* bloomer.

"You sure you weren't going around and talking to the other students in our class, too, Ludie?"

Now that I thought about it, I felt like the girls still wouldn't have treated me like normal.

She didn't deny it, but her lack of response gave me my answer.

"Well, then. Thank you, too, Ludie."

"...Mm-hmm. But it wasn't just me and Iori, either, you know?"

At this, she looked out in front of us. Standing there was a girl with pink pigtails—Katarina. She glanced at Ludie and walked straight up to me. She seemed like she was just the tiniest bit annoyed.

"Listen, you. How many more times are you going to make a mess of things before you're satisfied? Hmm?"

I was pretty sure Katarina had already seen the bulletin board and learned the truth.

"I don't really remember doing anything that bad?"

"*Ugh*, geez. Well, do whatever you want, I don't care. Pretty amazing stuff. Admirable, even. But you know what? You need to consider everyone around you a bit more, got it?" she said, raising a finger and pressing it firmly into my chest.

"Do you have any idea how worried Ludie and the others were for you? How much they wanted to help you out?"

".......I mean, I'm really, really, grateful for all that."

Ludie couldn't hold back her laughter as Katarina groaned and scratched her head in confusion.

"Kousuke? The truth is, Rina was really, really worried about you, too. She seemed ready to fly off the handle whenever your name came up and was insistent about you not being the person the rumors made you out to be."

Then Katarina's eyes popped wide open, and she drew in close to Ludie in a panic.

"Wh-what? Ludie! What're you going on about? Like I would ever be all worked up over a stupid idiot like him!"

Seeing Katarina's slightly pink cheeks, I couldn't hold back my smile. Though, thanks to that, she sent a real sharp glare my way.

"Sorry for making you anxious. And, well, I owe you one and then some."

"*Tch!*" Katarina clicked her tongue and crossed her arms. Then she stepped away from me and leaned up against a nearby wall.

"...Well, it's just, there's all these rumors going around, all about you. You know about them, right?"

"Very familiar, unfortunately."

"See, like, I know you're not that type of guy, so, it's just...just really annoying."

Katarina sighed quietly. "A real bunch of conceited jerks those guys are, if you ask me. Labeling people they barely even know and looking down on other people like that. And then with this whole exam thing... It seriously pissed me off," Katarina said before heaving a big sigh. "So, listen, there's something I want to ask you..."

"What's that?" I asked.

"Do you still think...that I'll get strong enough to stand shoulder-to-shoulder with you?"

The answer was obvious.

"Uh, of course you will? Everyone's gonna leave me in the dust if I'm not careful. That's why I'm climbing as high as I can with everything I've got."

"...Oh yeah?"

Katarina had something on her mind. I was able to figure out for the most part what she was thinking. As for what I could do for her...

"Oh right, so, there's this dungeon I know, it's pretty tough. Well, I was able to clean it up without much trouble, but for you, Katarina... Well, anyway, what do you say? Wanna try taking it down?"

"*Excuse* me?"

I purposefully goaded Katarina. I had absolutely no intentions of directing her to a dungeon she'd be unsuited for. If anything, I wanted to introduce her to the most suitable challenges to help her grow even stronger.

Katarina shot a dubious glance at me. Before she could say anything, Ludie began to speak.

"Rina. I think it's a good idea."

Katarina stared hard at Ludie a moment until she finally turned her eyes away and fixed them on me.

"If Ludie says so......Fine, I guess I could head there. If I need to kill some time, or something."

"Yeah, I think you should check it out."

If she was going to surpass me, she could go right ahead—I didn't mind. Not that I planned on letting her.

"Ugh, what's with you! Drives me nuts."

Then she suddenly lowered her voice.

"Seriously, I'm not gonna let you or Iori beat me."

She threw a pointed look my way.

"I'll admit you got the skills and potential, that's for sure."

Rina Katou, main heroine. She was strong. I knew that very well. I was going to make sure she'd get that powerful, too. But I wasn't going to lose, either.

"Thanks, I guess. In that case, go ahead and enjoy that inflated ego while it lasts," she said, before turning her back to us. Then, waving her arms as she went, she walked off toward the school building. As I watched her go, a thought came to me.

"Yo, Katarina!"

"What?"

As she turned around, I tossed a ring to her.

"Thanks for everything. That's my thank-you. Go ahead and use it."

When we arrived at the magical bulletin board, a crowd of students had already gathered. Noise and chatter filled the area, but as people began laying eyes on me, silence spread through the crowd like the ripples from a rock tossed into a pond. I took in everyone's stares.

Then, only a few breaths later, a hush enveloped the scene.

Everyone directed their gaze toward us. Ignoring all the other students, we moved into a position where we'd be able to see the bulletin board. As we did, the people in front of us split to the left and right, parting like the Red Sea to form a path.

In the middle of our approach, someone whispered:

"That's Kousuke Takioto."

It was a bit funny. In spite of all the students near the top of the ranking getting super high marks on the exam, I had a big fat goose egg. Looking just at the total score, I had far and away the lowest grades in school. And yet, I was seated right at the top of the class.

The highest-scoring first-years listed who I'd already met were Ludie and Iori. It looked like Iori had put in a lot of effort, because he'd placed fifth overall. For a protagonist on the first playthrough, that was a pretty good spot to be.

As the three of us chatted and headed back, a voice calling my name resounded from the now stony-silent area.

"Kousuke!"

Weaving through the crowd to meet us was Iori. It appeared he had come to check the scores, too.

RANKING BOARD

1 KOUSUKE TAKIOTO

ROYAL

RANK	WRITTEN EXAM	PRACTICAL EXAM	TOTAL SCORE	LAYERS COMPLETED
	0 POINTS	0 POINTS	0 POINTS	40 LAYERS SOLO

2 GABRIELLA EVANGELISTA

RANK	WRITTEN EXAM	PRACTICAL EXAM	TOTAL SCORE	LAYERS COMPLETED
	96 POINTS	84 POINTS	180 POINTS	- LAYERS

3 LUDIVINE MARIE-ANGE DE LA TRÉFLE

RANK	WRITTEN EXAM	PRACTICAL EXAM	TOTAL SCORE	LAYERS COMPLETED
	84 POINTS	92 POINTS	176 POINTS	- LAYERS

"Congrats on the taking the top rank! Sheesh, Kousuke, you really are amazing."

Seeing Iori with a big, full-faced smile soothed me. When I thought about it, I really owed him a lot. Before I could thank him for it, though...

"Hey Iori, why don't we go somewhere else?"

I didn't want him to get wrapped up in the awestruck eyes around us. As we walked, I started to talk with him.

"I heard you really did a lot for me, huh? Thanks for that."

When I said this, Iori broke into a bashful smile and scratched his cheek.

"You're welcome... But I wish you would've explained everything to me first. I mean, I was super worried when you didn't show up for our exams, you know! At first, I thought maybe you had gotten sick or something."

I'd made a huge blunder. If I knew I was going to make him this worried, I would've laid out everything to him beforehand.

"Still, I was surprised. I mean, you didn't come to school at all, but you really did snag the top rank."

I broke into a smile. He was right in that it would normally be an inconceivable outcome.

"Well, what did I tell you? I said I'd come out on top."

"Yeah, you did."

"Besides, you did pretty dang incredible yourself, I mean, fifth? If I actually took the exams, a score like that'd be absolutely impossible for me."

I wouldn't fail exactly, but...well... The just-bad-enough-to-have-a-hard-time-saying-it-aloud type of score wasn't out of the question.

"I mean, yeah, I guess most people would say it's an impressive score. But you know, then I had this thought."

"What sort of thought?"

"That you really are amazing for focusing solely on growing stronger and staying true to yourself, despite all the negative looks you got from everyone else. But also, that I still want to surpass you, too."

He looked at me, a serious expression on his face.

He wanted to top me, huh? Well, Iori, depending on how things played out, it was absolutely possible. However...

"Oh yeah? Well, I don't have any plans on giving up my place at the top, buddy," I said before giving a big grin.

Go ahead and try if you think you're up to snuff. I was going to keep on running ahead, too far ahead for you to catch up, and stand at the pinnacle as the strongest in the world.

"Yeah, I wouldn't have it any other way."

We both laughed. That's when it happened.

"Oh, big broooo!"

Both Iori and I jumped at the sound of the voice.

"Wh-whaaaaaat?! Wh-why are you here?!"

We'd both reacted for entirely different reasons. Iori was flustered about why the person who'd addressed us was there, while I was reacting to hearing a voice that had taken care of me many times, and in all sorts of different ways, in real life.

"Yup, I'm here! A bunch of stuff happened, and I ended up transferring! ♪"

She made an adorable display of sticking out her tongue and cocking her head slightly to the side. What a flirt.

Well, then. It was finally time for her to make her entrance. I knew she'd be showing up eventually.

"Oh, wait, were you in the middle of something?"

She turned toward me and bowed slightly.

"Sorry!"

"Oh, no, don't worry about it. No need to bow. Nice to meet you. I'm Iori's friend and classmate, name's Kousuke Takioto. She's Ludivine, and this—"

"I'm Master Kousuke's fully devoted and supremely beautiful maid, Nanami."

There were a litany of ways I would've liked to have responded to that, but now wasn't really the time. Yup, and the other girl's face tightened up for a second there.

When I glanced over at Ludie, she seemed confused by this new girl's sudden appearance. It made sense, really. Meanwhile, it was all too normal for Nanami to throw out strange and obtuse jokes like this.

"Oh, sorry. I didn't introduce myself."

The girl gave a tiny bow. Then, with slightly upturned eyes, she looked at me, tilting her head and making a show of pulling the bangs, hanging over her eyes, back behind her ear. Finally, she flashed a big, toothy grin while looking up at me at an angle.

Yup, she sure was a flirt all right. But that coquettish element to her behavior was so true to character that it put me at ease.

Well then, if I was going to get more involved with Iori, that meant I'd be getting to know this girl, too.

She was one of the main heroines on the *Magical★Explorer* box art, capable of wielding power on par with Ludie—Iori's little sister.

"I'll be transferring here. I'm Iori's younger stepsister, Yuika Hijiri! I'm looking forward to getting to know everyone!"

—Yukine's Perspective—

"My, my, my... An emergency Three Committees meeting?" Shion murmured, amused. Despite being summoned on short notice, she looked to be in good spirits.

"I figured as much. It seems my prediction was correct," Fran chimed in, adjusting her glasses.

"Did you know things would play out like this then, Yukine?"

"Yeah."

I pulled out my Tsukuyomi Traveler and checked the rankings that had just been released.

"No matter how many times I look at it, I just can't believe my eyes."

"I agree. Not even we could manage a clear time that short. What sort of strategy did he use to pull it off?"

The word *earth-shattering* had never been more appropriate.

He'd become the talk of the Academy. In fact, he was the *only* thing they were talking about on campus. Outside of the girls popular enough to have their own fan clubs, had there been anyone else who had become so widely gossiped about?

The first-year class rankings kicked it all off. Some of the people who saw it spread the word. Later that evening, the entire school was informed when a notification about the new record went out to everyone's Tsukuyomi Traveler.

The record was out of this world. Far too strange. Forty whole layers was totally ridiculous. But above all, it was the fact that he did it in just seven days, and totally solo, that sent shivers down our spines.

The majority of the second- and third-year students who saw the text had probably figured it was an incorrect announcement or some sort of technical glitch. However...

Takioto had actually pulled it off.

After learning it was true, the upperclassmen and teachers were even more flabbergasted than the first-years.

The older students were painfully aware of how hard it was to reach the fortieth layer. It wasn't someplace you got to overnight. Our party had struggled to get that far, even with President Monica in our ranks. Right now, Takioto might've been able to beat the boss on the fortieth layer, but I had figured the route to the final layer would make him throw in the towel. Seeing him pull off such an incredible feat, a thought came to me.

"I want to surpass President Monica and become the strongest in the Academy."

I wanted to beat her. Outmatch her and claim my spot at the top. Then, as the Academy's strongest, I wanted to stand before Takioto and face him.

Because I knew he was absolutely going to rise up that high.

"Yukine. Where did that come from? Wanting to beat President Monica all of a sudden?"

"I... While I still can, I want to become the strongest in the Academy."

I'd also made a promise to Suzune. But most of important of all, I wanted to remain Takioto's ultimate goal.

The room fell silent for a moment.

Fran didn't laugh, nor did she start teasing me. She stared at me, a solemn look on her face. Then...

"Ha-ha-ha, ha-ha-ha-ha!"

Suddenly, Shion burst into laughter.

"Oh, Yukine. That dream of yours will never come to be, I'm afraid." She closed her folding fan.

"Indeed, you may be able to outmatch the president, but strongest in the school? No, no, that will be quite impossible... Why, you ask? Well... Because the one claiming that honor will be *moi*," she asserted, standing in front of me.

"I shall admit, you are strong. Talented, as well. Be that as it may."

Her lips curved into an audacious grin.

"The thought I could possibly lose to you has never even crossed my mind. Not once."

She smiled like a predator licking their lips as they stared down their prey. I met this gaze of hers with my own.

Before either of us said another word, Fran spoke up.

"What are you two going on about?"

We turned to her at the same moment.

"Are the both of you forgetting that I'm standing right here?"

"Fran...," Shion muttered.

"I think you both possess top-class talent and ability, far above average. And I'm sure you'll be able to become talented leaders who will guide the Academy forward and grow even stronger."

Fran pushed her glasses up her nose and gave a small sigh. Then, she shifted her sights to me. She stared directly into my eyes.

"Right now, Yukine, I can sense a resolve in you that I've never felt before. Shion, I know that since you've joined the Ceremonial Committee, you've been putting in twice as much effort as anyone else."

Fran closed her eyes, taking a deep breath.

"But your dramatic progress of late is intolerable. I wonder when it all started...... Probably around when that dungeon appeared in town. You changed a bit, Yukine, and seeing that, Shion, you've started to head into dungeons more frequently, too..."

"Fran?"

"For me, you're both my goal, in some ways. Shion, you have a constant ambition to get ahead in the world and grow stronger. Yukine, you're so rigorous with your training, never letting yourself get complacent. And the fruits of both of your hard work are reflected in your skills."

No, Shion wasn't the only one. Fran was the same way.

"Hold on, Fran. You're pouring everything you've got into tackling dungeons alongside your Student Council work."

While she dived into dungeons together with President Monica, training with her and learning from her along the way, she deftly handled her responsibilities at the Academy. She was extremely diligent, and on top of that...she was talented. Talented enough to make me worry she might pass me by.

"What in heaven's name are you blathering about? You are *just* as much my rival, too. I haven't once taken you lightly."

Indeed, Fran was strong.

Looking askance at Shion as she smiled, Fran added, "Though I am still the strongest, naturally," before a gentle smile came to her face as well.

"That's right. I'm taking each day as seriously as I can. I'm getting plenty stronger, too. So..."

She opened her eyes and stared hard at the two of us.

"I don't plan on losing to you two, either. If you're both going to become the strongest in school, then I'll overcome you both and get even more powerful than that," Fran said, adjusting the position of her glasses. Then...

"Let's go. I need to finish up my preparations for the meeting before the committee presidents all show up."

She walked off.

It was another twenty minutes before the meeting preparations were finished and the committee presidents came together.

There were several quick knocks, and a single girl came into the meeting room.

"It appears I'm the last to get here... Oh no, not quite the last," Student Council President Monica said, looking over the gathered faces.

In this room sat the president of the Morals Committee, Captain Stef; the president of the Ceremonial Committee, Ceremonial Minister Benito, and his vice president, Vice-Ceremonial Minister Shion; as well as Student Council Vice President Fran; the newly arrived Student Council President Monica; and me.

With this, all the presidents and vice presidents of the Three Committees had come together.

There was one other person who was supposed to be here, but she often showed up late. President Monica knew this and was ready to start.

Seeing everyone take their seats, Fran placed the cup of coffee she'd prepared in front of President Monica.

"Now then, the reason for this emergency meeting......probably goes without saying, right?"

"Gotta be about him, right?" Minister Benito said with a laugh. Everyone here was well aware of today's subject.

"Kousuke Takioto. Entered the Tsukuyomi Academy Dungeon the

moment it was unlocked. He cleared the second-years' target goal of forty layers solo, and in only a week, too. I can't find any other word besides 'freaky' to describe it."

Fran pushed her glasses up, then passed out the documents she'd been holding.

The files contained Takioto's personal information. However...

"What's all this, then? Almost everything about him is 'unknown.' Is this even worth looking at?"

"We could pretty much say the same for you, Saint Stefania."

At Monica's reply, Captain Stef tossed the paper away and leaned back in her chair. Then she brought a cup of coffee to her lips.

Though she typically put on an innocent persona, Captain Stef would let her actual harsh and biting personality come out in the company of her peers. If any of the students outside the Three Committees saw this drastic change in her, they'd definitely be disillusioned. Conversely, if they saw Minister Benito as he was among the other committee presidents, the best at reading the room and being considerate, his bad reputation on campus would vanish in an instant.

"Yes, but seeing it written down makes the information easier to remember than just hearing it verbally, wouldn't you agree?"

Fran didn't say anything more than that, but I could imagine how she would've added something like: *Given that he possesses a number of unique characteristics.*

Academy student information was released to the Three Committees, to a certain extent. Without treading too far into their private lives, of course.

However, there were select individuals who had even less information provided, with only the bare minimum about them made available. Such situations were common when it came to each countries' VIPs and their children.

An imperial princess like Ludie probably had just as little information available as Takioto.

Monica cleared her throat with a cough.

"The information's been handed out. Now then, we need to discuss what we need to do first."

"Words of warning to the other first-years, I'd say!" Minister Benito said, amused.

"I can just imagine a mighty flood of imbeciles spewing all sorts of nonsense about being able to do the same thing themselves," Shion said, fanning herself. Her smile as she spoke was all too like her.

"'If he can do it, I can do it!' Oh yes... Very easy to imagine, isn't it? ♪"

Benito was right; there was bound to be a fair number of students thinking that. But if that led to the absolute worst-case scenario......
It was too horrible to imagine.

"That said, it would be a terrible idea to have our Ceremonial Committee say that. I'll leave that in your hands, Student Council."

"Right, of course. There'd probably be even more of them jumping right into the dungeon if you were the one to tell them off, Benito," Monica said with a smile.

"Right? I suppose we'll just have to exercise some restraint in our activities, then."

The Ceremonial Committee members each gave a haughty laugh.

Suddenly, I wondered what the students would think if they saw the two of them peacefully conversing like this. They'd probably wonder what was actually going on with the Three Committees.

"Is it really necessary to stop them, I wonder?" Captain Stef chimed in. The laughter died out and the room went quiet. Shion and Fran sent fierce glares her way.

"What's the harm in letting them attempt to do the same? It'll serve as a good lesson, wouldn't you say?"

"And how, pray tell, do you plan on taking responsibility if a student then ends up dead, Saint Stefania?"

"I agree with Shion."

I couldn't hold back an exasperated sigh. While watching this back-and-forth, I was struck by the thought that Captain Stef was, without a doubt, the person most suited to be a member of the Ceremonial Committee. Though she'd ended up in our Committee because of her honor as a saint.

"Now, now, everyone. Let's settle down and enjoy this delicious coffee, okay? Did you brew this fine cup for us, Fran?"

"Yes, I did. It makes me happy to hear you say that, Minister Benito."

Anyone would be happy to hear a compliment from a gourmet palate like Benito's.

"There's such an elegant fragrance to Fran's coffee, isn't there.........?
Why don't you enjoy some yourself, Stefania? Also, while you do indeed

have a point, perhaps there might be a bit kinder way of getting it across, wouldn't you say?"

"The Student Council will handle reminding the other first-years not to attempt any unreasonable trips into the dungeon. As a precaution, we'll request support from the Morals and Ceremonial Committees, too. Thanks in advance."

Things were close to getting out of hand, but Minister Benito immediately calmed things down. President Monica then quickly moved to change the subject.

"The next issue, then, is how we're going to deal with Kousuke."

"Hmmm, well, he's definitely getting recommended to join the Three Committees. I heard some of the rumors before coming, which made me consider it, and personally, I'd say the Ceremonial Committee would be the best fit. Though I'd love to have him come join us, instead."

"Well, that's all up to him now, isn't it? We're in a bit of a special position, after all. Though, should he not choose our Committee, I'm still quite intrigued, myself. I'd like him to join one of the Committees, at the very least," Shion said, opening up her fan, then covering her mouth with it as she stared toward me. President Monica was also looking my way.

Shion and President Monica had previously seen Takioto and me charge into a dungeon together to rescue Ludie. This was Shion, though, so she was obviously just grinning to tease me for being so friendly with him.

Actually, all the members gathered in here likely had looked into things enough to know Takioto and I had a friendly relationship.

"Wouldn't the Ceremonial Committee be difficult? No doubt his abilities warrant it. But, what about the necessary social authority?"

Captain Stef sounded a little annoyed as she spoke, likely because Takioto's actions seemed like they'd lead to more work for her.

"I'd say the Morals Committee would be just as tough a fit, wouldn't you? I've heard he almost never attends class. The way he behaves, he'd destroy the Moral Committee's basic principles. If we were to invite him into a Committee, then...... The Student Council, maybe?" Fran mused as she passed her eyes over the documents she'd prepared.

"Well, how about we ask someone who might have an answer?"

President Monica turned to me, taking everyone else's attention with her.

I'd been staying quiet on purpose, but she went and asked me directly, so I decided to respond only with what I felt it was okay to talk about.

"I think Takioto could manage to fit in any of the three. He's a pretty serious person at heart."

Putting aside which one he may have wanted to join, I felt that if Takioto put his mind to it, he could fit into any one of the Committees.

"But the Ceremonial Committee requires social standing, too. He'd had a really tough time without it."

President Monica was right.

"That's definitely not something to worry about it. If anyone tried laying a hand on him, they'd essentially be picking a fight with several countries at once. His guardian's here at the school, too."

"Oooh, really now? Picking a fight with multiple countries? Now that'd mean he's a VIP on the level of our Acting Saint or Princess Ludivine. Such an important person, behaving like that……? Wait, I get it…… But, oh no, no, that couldn't possibly be it."

Minister Benito seemed to have figured it out.

"She'll be here shortly, so go ahead and ask her yourself."

"Wait, coming here?! No, are you saying what I think you're saying?!"

The timing was perfect. As if on cue, the woman in question walked into the room.

"Sorry for running late, everyone."

Academy Principal Marino Hanamura made her entrance.

"I can guess what an emergency meeting might be about, but what's the topic at hand?"

I answered her.

"Takioto."

Chuckling dryly, Marino took her seat, before she…

"Yuuuup, just what I thought. Isn't my little boy just incredible?"

…totally dropped a bomb on everyone.

As soon as the words left her mouth, I could sense a chill descend over the room.

They couldn't have known, really.

"Yes, Kousuke Takioto is a member of the *Hanamura family*."

Everyone was at a loss for words. Even Fran's jaw was half open.

However, there was one other girl besides Marino and me who didn't look any different from normal.

President Monica sighed slightly and turned her attention to me. She was the only person to remain as composed as usual, in total contrast to the atmosphere in the room.

"Yukine. Let me ask you, then. What sort of person is Kousuke Takioto, anyway? You know him pretty well, don't you? I want to hear it in your own words."

At the question, I suddenly thought to myself.

Just what sort of person was he? A hard worker, a student, an idiot sometimes, trustworthy for the most part, despite the occasional indecent glimmer in his eyes. Above all else, he cared deeply for others. Also, he liked matcha just like I did, was surprisingly good at cooking, always fun to be around.........

Pfft! What in the world was going through my head?

Clearly, those weren't the sentiments Student Council President Monica was looking for.

Kousuke Takioto...

He was a strange guy. It felt like he looked at the world from a different point of view than the rest of us. Just what sort of world did he see? I wondered if I could behold the same world he did if I stood where he stood. I wanted to get a glimpse of that world of his.

Though little more than a hunch, I got the sense it wasn't a world dazzling bright with money and riches.

I felt like his was vast and brimming with beautiful flowers. Together with a splendid waterfall and a stream below.

Suddenly, I recalled what had happened at that waterfall.

I remembered the words Takioto said to me there. Hadn't he told me the same thing inside a dungeon? Or when he had been hassled by the LLL fan club students?

Right. The perfect response to Monica's question was right there. Takioto had said as much himself plenty of times by now.

It was something that sounded like nonsense to anyone who didn't know him. Side-splitting absurdity. In the past, they were words everyone had laughed off. But things were different now. It was a declaration I felt would come true.

The fact that these words floated into my mind, and that I thought they actually suited him, were sure signs I had been corrupted by him, too.

But I didn't hate the feeling at all. It was rather pleasant, and despite the corrupting influence, I was happy. And I was already too far gone; for now, I was hoping even more of his bad influence would wash over me.

That settled it. I knew what I was going to say. If I was going to say it, though, I should take the chance to really play the part. The words were so very much like him, it was only fair to try delivering them just like he would.

Takioto's face appeared in my mind. Right, during really important moments like this, he'd say it like it was nothing, brimming full of absolute confidence.

"Kousuke Takioto......"

At that moment, turning my face toward the strongest student in the school, Student Council President Monica, I flashed a dauntless smile.

"...is the guy who's going to be the strongest in the Academy."

Good day. Iris here, back again after being out of touch for a bit.

There's now an official Twitter account. The plan is to post back-and-forths with Nanami, along with other content. I'd greatly appreciate it if you could follow it here: https://twitter.com/Majieku_ (@Majieku_)

—Acknowledgments—

Thank you, as always, Kanatuki-sensei. Ms. Ruija, Yuika, Fran, Shion. All of their designs are absolutely perfect, top to bottom. Yukine's illustrations were also truly stunning. Especially the one showing her Nine-Headed Dragon; I nearly had a heart attack the instant I saw it.

Next, to Higa-sensei and your handling of the manga adaptation. The vibrant and lively way you drew Takioto is quite fantastic! I can't wait to read the next chapter......!

Next, to Fumiaki Maruto-sensei, Romeo Tanaka-sensei, and Yuui-chirou Higashide-sensei and the comments you gave me. It made me so happy just knowing such prominent members of the eroge industry are reading my work, and I was so deeply moved to receive your feedback on top of that. Especially as a long-time fan of all of your works... It made me feel really glad to be a light novel author. Even now, it still feels like I'm living the dream.

For Mr. Kai Sugiyama and his book design. Thank you for your typically wonderful work. The Windows OS look, the arrows, the game-UI-like design—I love it all!

I'd also like to extend my gratitude to those involved with the MAD promotional video, the members of ave;new/ave;new project, Mr. Yashiro Kanzuki, Lump of Sugar Ltd, and everyone else who helped out. After watching *the* Kishimen intro over and over and over again, I never would have thought that I'd get to do a collab with it someday... I truly couldn't be happier.

To my editor, Miyakawa. Thank you not only for your usual manuscript checks and proofreading, but also for coordinating the video production and so much more. There is one thing that's been on my mind, though. You see, I still get work emails from you over the weekend, and even when I call you up late at night, you're still usually plugging away, right? Don't keel over on me, now. If you're put out of commission, then that'll spell the end of *Magical ★ Explorer*, too.

Finally. To all the readers who purchased this book. You have my humblest gratitude. I have you all to thank for where I am right now. I hope you'll continue to come along with me on this journey.

—Everything Else—

This is a personal matter, but there's something I'd like your advice on today.

When your pal Iris here writes descriptions, I often do an image search on the Internet.

Take scenery, for instance. If I'm going to describe nature in detail, then I really do want to write while referencing the scenery in question. When possible, I'll even go out to that location, or a similar one in person (though when I dedicate too many words to these, they end up first on the editing chopping block).

For this volume, one description in particular was quite important. Now that you've read it for yourself, I'm sure you all know what I'm referring to.

Yes, that's right—the panties' descriptions.

It's so obvious that you didn't really need to mull over it for long, did you? I mean, if I'm not going to go all out describing girls' undergarments, then what else in the world was worth the effort? With that in mind, what exactly was I supposed to do to experience them myself?

Now, the option of asking an acquaintance to show me their panties straight-up, like a blazing fastball right down the middle, was certainly there. But not only could that fastball come flying back at me, the pitcher, I was also just as likely to get a baseball bat across the nose with it. If worse came to worst, I could end up being blasted in the media for it.

In that case, what could I do? I've mentioned the solution already—an Internet search. How convenient a tool it is for allowing men to gaze on lovely panties from the safety of their homes.

However, this comes with a very, very, *very* big drawback. As I imagine many of you are already aware (and those who've been reading the web novel likely know that I've complained about this before), those activities are actually recorded in your search and browsing history, and you'll be shown recommended products based on them. I'm sure you can guess what happened to Iris here after looking up pictures of panties nonstop.

That's right, I started seeing nothing but underwear ads online.

But that doesn't really bother me. I don't mind it at all. My adolescent niece could look at me like a weirdo, wondering why my web pages are filled with panties ads, and I wouldn't give it a second thought.

However, in one of the ads that popped up with my browsing history was something far more enticing, dangerously so. I had searched for it, so it wasn't very strange for it to show up. Items so cute and precious you want to squeeze them tight.

I'm talking about P*kemon plushies, of course.

Honestly, I managed to get through the web pages plastered with panties, but things weren't so easy with the P*kemon plushies.

As soon as I'd catch those cute, round eyes looking my way, I'd go and snuggle up against those soft cheeks. When those P*kemon plushies were showing up in my web page ads, those eyes of theirs would plead with me. "Forge a pact with me. Let's become P*kemon masters!"

However, I am but a humble man, past thirty. In the past, I'd have a grand time playing the games with my young nieces and nephews, but now they throw me looks that seem to say, *Ew, you're over thirty and still into P*kemon?* They simply don't know the truth that no matter how much time may go by, we'll always be P*kemon trainers at heart (beautifully put, if I do say so myself).

Really though, I don't care about judging looks from children. I need to save money and look to the future. I'm doing everything I can to scrape together my vital light novel and video game funds. Any more, and I'll need to eat into my food and living expenses to make do. However, I'd like to avoid that if possible. That's precisely why I'm holding out with my will of steel! Now then… After coming this far, I'm sure you've guessed what exactly I'd like all your advice on.

Yes, it's exactly what you're thinking.

I've got way too many plushies in my room, so where would it be best to store them all?

I guess I should just freeload at my editor's house, right?

Irisu

Personally, I think the Kousuke/Nanami combo is the best of them all.

神楽門
(Noboru Kannatuki)

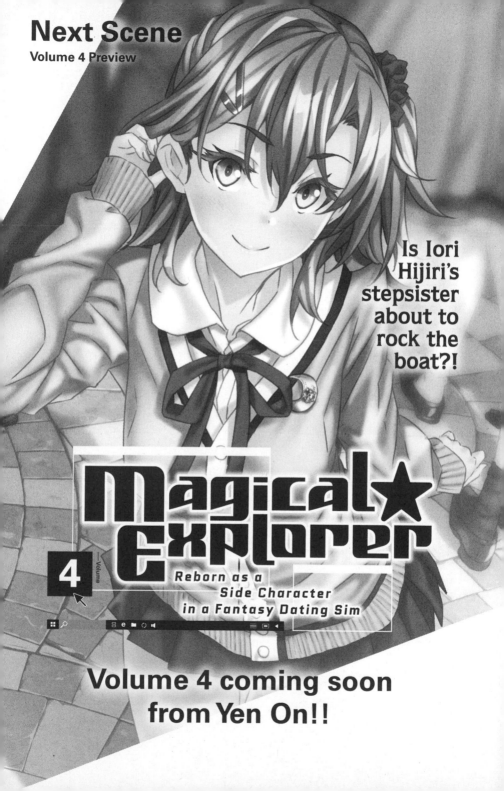

Next Scene
Volume 4 Preview

Is Iori Hijiri's stepsister about to rock the boat?!

Magical★Explorer

4 —Volume

Reborn as a
Side Character
in a Fantasy Dating Sim

Volume 4 coming soon
from Yen On!!